KINGPIN WIFEYS

SEASON 3 VOLUME 8

BY K. ELLIOTT

Copyright © 2018 by Urban Lifestyle Press
P.O. Box 12714
Charlotte, NC 28220
http://www.kelliottonline.com/

Copyright 2018 by http://www.kelliottonline.com/.

All rights reserved.

No part of this book may be used or reproduced in any manner whatsoever without written permission. For information, address Urban Lifestyle Press, P.O. Box 12714 Charlotte, NC 28220 http://www.kelliottonline.com/

This ebook is licensed for your personal enjoyment only. This ebook may not be re-sold or given away to other people. If you would like to share this book with another person, please purchase an additional copy for each recipient. If you're reading this book and did not purchase it, or it was not purchased for your use only, then please return to Amazon.com and purchase your own copy. Thank you for respecting the hard work of this author.

April   2018

Contents

KINGPIN WIFEY III,

Part 1: Thicker Than Blood

Agent Daniels stood between the lifeless bodies of Black and Agent Malarkey. FBI agents Mark Dumas and David Mackins arrived at the scene in a dark blue Ford transit van five minutes after Daniels radioed in the words "officer down." Dumas was the driver; Mackins rode shotgun, both were part of Daniels's posse. A Honduran by the name of Francisco Valdez was hogtied and gagged; Lay on the floor in the back of the van. Days earlier the agents had robbed Valdez of two thousand kilos of heroin.

For two days they had tortured the man, gouging his eyes with pens, burning his ass cheeks with hot irons, trying to get him to give up his connect. The agents wanted to rob the connect because they knew that there were more drugs somewhere. Valdez wouldn't talk. He said that his whole family would be murdered if he sold out his connect, and for that reason, he had to die. Valdez was a slim Hispanic man with a full head of curly hair. He was wearing a pair of gray soccer sweat pants and a pair of light blue Adidas running shoes. Dumas and Mackins dragged him out of the van. Valdez had refused to give them the information, and now it was time to pay.

After Dumas and Mackins dragged Valdez out of the van, Mackins removed the gag from Valdez's mouth.

Daniels said, "Are you ready to talk?"

Valdez looked up at Daniels and spat on his leg. "Fuck you. I'd rather die than put my family at risk."

 Daniels blasted him in the back of the head."Valdez's brains oozed from the side of his head. The story would be that Valdez met Daniels and Malarkey for an undercover buy. Valdez suspected that they were the police. Valdez shot Malarkey and Daniels shot Valdez.

Daniels didn't feel good about killing Agent Malarkey, but he had to go. Mark Dumas had found out from an informant that

Malarkey had been pinched and he had planned to give Daniels up. Once they put out the story that Valdez shot Agent Malarkey and that Daniels had shot Valdez, Daniels would be a hero. They would later load Black's body in the back of the van and dump it off on the side of the highway. People would figure the LA boys killed him, or the Detroit boys, or possibly some gangsters from Atlanta. Black had a lot of enemies. It was important for Daniels to cover this up. If word got around that he had murdered Black, none of the Atlanta gangsters that were paying him would ever trust him.

***

It was 6:32 a.m. when Q heard a knock on the door. He hopped out of the bed and slid into a pair of blue shorts. The knocking was getting louder. It was probably the concierge or perhaps the trash valet. They sometimes knocked to see if he had any trash. There was more knocking. He heard voices, but he couldn't make out what they were saying. The valet had never knocked this aggressively.

He dashed through the rooms and when he opened the door, there were three police officers. Two plainclothes and a uniformed cop. Q recognized the black uniformed officer, from the time when he had come to his house for threatening Terrell, the basketball player who had been trying to see Starr. The two plainclothes were white.
One of the white cops stepped forward, He looked to be around thirty. He had brown hair, blue eyes, and a pleasant, clean-shaven face.
Q eyed the black cop and said, "What is the problem?"
"We have a warrant for your arrest."
Q's eyebrows rose and then he looked at the black cop. "Is this about the communicating a threat charge on Terrell's punk ass?"
The black man said, "No, that issue has been resolved."
"Okay, I'm confused."
The young officer presented Q with the warrant and said, "Mr. Mills, you're under arrest for conspiracy to murder."

2

"Murder who?"

"Trey Carter."
"What? This is straight up bullshit and ya'll know ya'll ain't got nothing on me."
The black officer removed his cuffs from his belt and said, "I'm going to need for you to turn around."
Q turned around without a fight. What was he supposed to do? He was outnumbered.
The man placed the cuffs on Q's wrists and said, "Tell me if these are too tight."
Q said, "This is some bullshit."
The third officer who had been quiet said, "You'll have your chance to tell your side of the story."
"I don't have shit to say until I hire an attorney. Can I get some shoes? I can't go downtown with only socks."Q said.
The black man led Q to the bedroom and he slid into a pair of Nikes. Then they hauled his ass down to the station.

***

Two days after Black's funeral, Shamari used his sister's car to drive down to Black's father's junkyard. Bankhead Bo, shirtless and wearing blue and white pajama bottoms, stepped out onto the porch.

A freckled-faced white woman named Becca stood up and said, "Bo, you need to put your shirt on. It's chilly out here."
He turned to her and snarled, "Woman, it's the middle of April."
"It's still chilly."
"Look, woman, I call the shots 'round here. Not you."
 He stared at Shamari and said, "Do I know you?"
"Yeah, I'm Black's friend."
"Black? Black ain't got no friends now. Black in the ground."
"Well, I'm his friend to the end."

Becca disappeared into the house and came back outside with a T-shirt. She tried to hand it to Bo, but he refused it.

"I done told you I ain't wearing no shirt."

Becca stepped back inside.

Bo said, "I know you. You're the red boy that was with Jr. that night we had to dispose of that body.

"Yeah."

"The English professor."

"Huh?"

"The one correcting my English."

Shamari laughed.

"What can I help you with?"

"Just checking on you."

"I mean I don't know what to tell you 'cept this isn't the way life is supposed to happen. I ain't 'posed to bury my kids. They are 'posed to bury me."Bo looked as if he wanted to cry and Shamari felt sorry for the man.

Bo sat on the porch and Shamari took a seat on the step below him.

"So, what happened? I been asking people and nobody seems to know what happened."

"What do you mean what happened? Ain't you his partna?"

"The day he got killed was the day I got out of prison."

Bo said, "One helluva coincidence."

"Hey, I didn't kill Black."

"I'm just sayin'."

"Don't say that."

"The truth is," Bo paused and said, "What the hell is yo name again?"

"Shamari."

"Mari."

"Yeah, that'll work."

"The truth is, Mari, I don't know who in the fuck killed my son, and that's a fucked up feeling. I heard he had been beefing with some dudes out of Detroit and somebody said he had some trouble with some niggas out of LA. I don't know."

"I don't want to go back to prison, but I have to get them. I owe Black that much."

Bo said, "We gotta get 'em."

Three months later, Shamari lay in the tiny bed in his sister's extra bedroom and stared at a club picture of him and Black. He remembered that night at Club Compound and, Black convinced twin sisters that they were producing a movie and they took the girls back to Black's home. Black sexed one of them and Shamari was about to screw the other, but he needed condoms. He didn't want to disturb Black, so he drove to the store. When he returned to his room, he found Black doggy styling "his" girl. Black's excuse: "Bruh! I couldn't tell them apart."Legitimate excuse except, they weren't even identical. Shamari laughed, thinking about him. Damn, he missed Black.

Shamari had been free from prison for a few months now. He and Jada were on good terms, but she had made it clear that she was enjoying her single life and didn't want a relationship with him. For now, he lived with his sister and her piece-of-shit-boyfriend, Hunch. He staggered out of bed, did a quick set of fifty pushups, and then kissed the pic of Black. He pointed to the sky and said, "I know you looking down on me, big bruh, and I'm going to get revenge for you."

Hunch, barged into the room, wearing a tiny, dingy-ass shirt that struggled to cover his mountainous belly.

Shamari said, "Bruh, how many times I gotta tell you not to bust up in my room like that?"He wanted to slap the fuck out of Hunch but he couldn't and he didn't. Hunch was, after all, his sister's man.

"My bad, brother-in-law, but some dude out on the porch wanting to see you."

"Ty?"Ty was a dude that Shamari had met inside. He was released after doing fifteen years.

"No, it's not Ty. I 'member Ty. This dude taller than Ty and darker."

"Did he tell you his name?"

"Said his name was D."

"I don't know no motherfuckin' D. How does he look?"

"Bald. Dark. With a beard."

Shamari jumped up, grabbed his shirt that was lying on the bed and waltzed through the kitchen where his sister scrambled egg whites. He pecked her on the cheek.

Shamari looked back at Hunch and said, "Where the hell is D?"

"He's on the porch."

Shamari stepped onto the porch and spotted D. "Can I help you?"

"Need to talk to you."

"Man, first of all, how the fuck do you know me and why you coming over my sister's house?"

"It's about Black."

"You're a friend of Black?"

"Yes and no."

"Da fuck you mean?"

"Can you shut the door?"

"Bruh, this is my sister's house. Anything you gotta talk to me about, we can talk with the door open."

"I'm the one that got you out of prison."

"What?"

Daniels presented an FBI badge and ID.

"You're a Fed?"

"Please shut the door so we can talk."

Shamari slammed the door.

"Black and I were business partners."

"What?"

"I helped him. He helped me."

"What the fuck you mean? Black was a rat?"

"Not at all."

"Well, the only time I hear about somebody helping the police, they snitching."

"It's complicated."

"What?"

Daniels rocked from one leg to the other.

"What do you want?"

"I want to help you."

"Help me?"

"You're going to need money."

"I don't need money that bad."

"So, what? You think you're going to get a job?"

"A job? I ain't never had a job in my life and I ain't 'bout to get no job."

Daniels took a step forward and said, "This is how it worked. Homeland Security had an open investigation on Black and Dr. Craig Matthews recanted his statement on you. I made Black's investigation go away and I helped you get out of jail."

"For what price? What did it cost Black for this?"

"He helped me and I helped him."

"What does that supposed to mean?"

"Say I make a bust. I bust someone for a hundred kilos. Twenty-five of those kilos might get lost and find their way back on the street. That's where Black came in. I never once asked him what any other dealer was doing because I knew that he wouldn't help me, but he was smart enough to help himself."

"Good for him. Black was a pretty smart guy. I'm not as smart, though."

Daniels passed Shamari a business card.

Shamari said, "I won't need any card."He ripped the card in half.

***

Young Dolph's song PREACH blasted through Jada's fuchsia-colored Beats headphones. Jada stared in the mirror as she did a set of lunges with a pair of fifteen-pound dumbbells. She noticed a woman looking at her. This happened a lot when she came to the gym: admirers, Instagram followers, Snapchat followers, even women wanted to fuck her. She was used to the attention. After another set, the bitch was still staring. She sat the weights down and she was hoping that the headphones would deter the bitch from approaching because though she hated working out, listening to Trap Music motivated her. Young Dolph's song ended and PANDA came on by some artist named Designer, a knockoff version of Future. Although she

8

didn't know what the fuck he was saying, she had to admit the beat was banging. She did another set of lunges.

The woman approached and Jada thought the woman was a natural beauty, unlike Jada. Jada prided herself on her skin, but this woman's skin was flawless and her hair was natural. Jada took her as one of those chicks that washed their hair with juices and berries and gave herself facials with honey, unlike Jada who would rock the fuck out of a twenty-six-inch Brazilian weave and get a nip and tuck as needed to maintain. The woman had the most incredible teeth, and as Jada looked closely, she could tell that she had fillers. Perhaps, she wasn't so natural after all.
"I'm Jada."
"Ava."
Ava kept staring, almost with a lustful look. Jada had slept with women before, but she needed to be drunk. Right now she was completely sober.
"You come here often?"Ava asked.
"Not often enough. I rarely have time to make it to the gym."
"Job keeps you busy, huh?"
"Yes," Jada lied. Who the fuck was this ho' asking all these questions?
Jada said, "Nice to meet you, Ava, but I have to finish my workout."
"One more question."
"Yeah?"
"Can I have your number? Maybe we can hang out?"
"What?"
"Look, I'm not into girls, but I just moved here from Charlotte and I was looking for some cute chicks to hang out with."
Jada stared at country-ass Ava, wearing pink leggings and a sports bra that didn't even match. She wondered why of all the chicks in the gym, did she want to hang out with her.
"Ava, what kind of things are you into? I don't hand my number out to just anybody. Tell me about yourself. You're from Charlotte. What else?"
"I just got out of a bad relationship."
"Okay, haven't we all."

"It was REALLY bad. We ended up really hating each other."
"What was the problem?"
"He was broke."She paused. "I don't mean to come across like a gold digger, but I just can't deal with broke-ass dudes."
"Broke or just in a bad place?"
"Really broke. I mean he couldn't even take me to cheap-ass Olive Garden. The men I had dealt with before would fly me all over the world and we would do things, you know?"
"Well, we got that in common cuz I can't do broke either," Jada said.
"You look expensive."
"You're calling me a gold digger?"
"No, not at all."
"What do you mean by I look expensive?"
"You have a full face of makeup on at the gym. Body enhancements. Not throwing shade. I just don't think I can do surgery. I'm afraid of going to the hospital. I mean I had my teeth veneered, but that was it."
"I've heard I look expensive."
"Yes."
"You wanna hang out? Why?"
"You just seem like you will be a lot of fun."
"Are you sure you're not just looking for a man to take care of you?"
Ava smiled. That smile was too damn perfect.
"I mean, who don't want to meet rich men. I met a rich man on one of those Sugar Daddy sites."
"Yes."Jada had heard of the sites and had seen some of the members on the Steve Harvey show and decided there was no way in hell that she was going to sleep with some eighty-year-old man for a pair of Louboutins. She would use men, but with the exception of Big Poppa, she had to be attracted to the man. Even Big Poppa never got the kitty, although he did get to taste it.
"Yeah, I met a man on there, old Australian guy, owns a slew of private medical clinics. I would see him twice a month and he would pay my rent and give me spending money."
"And what did you have to do for him?"

"I'd fuck him a couple of times. He was a handsome man but then he wanted more and I couldn't see myself being with him in the long term."

Jada stared at her. She was telling all of her business. What kind of woman just meets a person at the gym and divulges so much information?

"Hey, Ava, I gotta go but follow me on Instagram. DM me and we can hang out."Jada didn't want to give Ava the number right now.

"What's your name?"

"@JadaSimone404."

"Cool. Nice meeting you, Jada."

***

The last time Jada had seen TeTe was at Black's funeral. TeTe greeted her with a hug and they went out to her patio and had Mojitos.

Jada said, "I love your outfit, Ms. Lady."

TeTe was wearing a white Armani pantsuits with black Manolo Blahniks.

"How are you feeling, lady?"Jada asked.

"You know I have good days and bad days. Sometimes, I think of some of the things he would say or do and I just bust out laughing. Sometimes I cry. I don't know if I will ever meet a man like that again."

"I know. He was special."

"I miss him so much, Jada."TeTe's eyes teared up and she thought about how life was going to be without Black and her sister Tessa. She hadn't had a chance to mourn her sister properly and when she received the news that Black had gotten murdered, she was devastated.

"It will take some time getting used to him not being here," Jada said.

"Right now, it hurts like hell."She sipped her drink. "You know I have a big personality and there aren't too many men that can take me."

Jada laughed and said, "Don't we know that."

11

"Black was a man's man. No woman could put him in place except his Nana. His Nana loved herself some Tyrann."

"I know."

TeTe disappeared into the house and returned with more drinks. She said to Jada, "I've never told anybody this but Black was working with the FBI."

Jada choked. "What do you mean, working?"

"There was this rogue Fed agent that was taking dope from dealers and traffickers and giving it to him. He would sell it and they would split the money."

"How do you know this?"

"Black told me everything."

Jada thought back to the day that Black had assured her that he didn't rob Fresh's connect. It must have been the FBI.

"I think that man had Black killed."

"Why?"

"I don't know. I just have a gut feeling that he wasn't killed by a gangster. Black was always careful."

"So no revenge for you, huh?"

"I didn't say all of that. My man got murdered, and he had enemies so I have to take care of that for him."

"You know that Black had a lot of people after him. Cali dudes. Detroit dudes." Jada then wondered if Fresh had something to do with it. He believed that Black had robbed his connect. Perhaps he knew about Black's murder.

"But I'm not understanding. If Black was getting product from the FBI dude, why would he want to kill Black?"

"I don't know. Perhaps Black wanted to stop being his partner. I don't know. This is information that Black took to the grave with him."

Jada and Starr sipped champagne as they sat in salon chairs at Happy Nails. Their feet were soaking in pedicure bowls. Jada liked to come to this place and she had invited Starr to come along. And she was glad that she had because though she loved the place, Mai, a young Vietnamese girl, always got in her damn business asking what she did for a living. When was she going to get married? Did she want to have children? Why didn't she have kids yet? She had answered the goddamned questions hundreds of times. Jada even stopped going but she could never quite arch her own eyebrows like Mai. The little Asian chick was placed on Earth to do eyebrows because every time Jada left, her brows were on fleek.

Mai was scrubbing Jada's feet and texting at the same time. Another girl, named Huang, was working on Starr's feet. Huang was pleasant and nosey but not quite as nosey as Mai.
"Q called today."
"What did he say?"
"Not a damn thing. I hung up."
"The nerve of that motherfucka'."
Jada sipped her champagne and said to Mai, "Would you pay attention to what you are doing and quit ear hustling? You're hurting my damn feet."
The woman looked confused. "Ear hustling? What you mean, Ms. Jada? Ear hustling?"
"Listening to some shit that ain't your damn business."
"Oh, ear hustling."She smiled, revealing huge, corn-colored teeth.
"I like that word. I use it."
"Pay attention to my feet."
Jada turned back to Starr and said, "I can't believe he had the nerve to try to call you."
"I know."
Jada said, "Wait a minute. Is he out?"

"No. He's on Wright Street."
"Is he going to be extradited sending him to Houston?"
"No, his trial is going to be in Georgia."
"I haven't heard from Fresh in a few months," Jada said.
"Damn."
"I don't care about him. I think I'm over him. I think I'm over dudes. I'm just trying to get myself together, you know?"
"What about the dude from Miami?"
Mai, still scrubbing Jada's feet, said to Starr. "I tell Ms. Jada that she need to get marry, settle down, have kids."
Jada wanted to do use her nosey ass with the champagne.
"Mai? What was the word we learned today?"
"Ear hustle."
"No, its ear hustling and you are doing it again."
"I sorry, Ms. Jada."
"Dude from Miami? Tank is his name. He got mad because one day he came over and Black was there and he accused me of fucking with Black."
Starr said, "Please! God bless the dead but I know there was no way in hell that you would fuck with Black."
Jada thought about the last time that she had seen Black. He had fucked her really good. Nobody would ever know that.
"Tank was married."
"And he's trying to tell you what to do?"
"That's men for you."
"Did you like him?"
"I did. I liked him a lot. I liked Fresh a lot, too. I like Shamari a lot."
"Out of the three. Who would you like to have been with the most?"
"Tough question, but I would say Fresh because even though me and Marl were together for a long time, there was just something missing. I still love him though. Tank is married so it would really be hard for me to trust him."
Jada received a call from an unrecognizable number. She answered the phone.
"Hello, Jada, it's Fresh. Can you meet me somewhere? It's important. I really need to see you."
She turned to Starr and said, "You have talked Fresh up."

***

Brooke entered Starr's office and said, "There is a man out there to see you."

"Did he tell you his name?"
"No. I asked but he wouldn't give it."
"How does he look?"
"Tall, dark, and handsome. Your type."
"What are you talking about, Brooke?"
"I know how you like them."She winked.
"Did he ask to see the manager?"
"No. He said that he wanted to see Starr."
Starr entered the showroom. A tall man wearing Tom Ford Aviators was there, dressed in brown Timberland wingtips, jeans and a designer T-shirt. His wavy hair was pulled into a ponytail. She didn't recognize him.
He said, "Damn, Starr. You are still the finest woman in any room," The man smiled revealing a bottom row of gold fronts.
"Do I know you?"
 He removed his glasses and she realized that she did know him. His name was Alan Green, aka Stunna. She'd known him since she was a kid. Before she started dating Trey, they had gone out a few times. He was from a family of gangsters, even his grandma had been a gangster. About twenty of them had gotten indicted by the Feds. They had all done time and gotten out and then got right back to dealing. Stunna had a sister named Micky—a hard-core dyke that dressed like a man. She and Starr were the same age and had gone to elementary school together. They had been on the same cheerleading squad and then around thirteen, she started acting and dressing like a boy. By high school, she was completely dyke. Micky and Stunna both dealt drugs as far back as she could remember.
She came out from behind the counter and hugged Stunna.
He stepped back and said, "Damn! You are so fine."He looked around the place and then asked, "Is this yours?"
"Yeah," she said proudly.
"You made it out of the hood."

"I did."
"Looks like you're doing well for yourself."
"It could be better, but business is doing well."Her cheekbones
raised and laugh lines emerged. She hadn't felt this good in a very
long time. Stunna's Bleu De Chanel cologne smelled tempting. A
good-smelling, dark man would get her every time.
"What brings you here and how did you know I was here?"
"I saw you at Black's funeral."
"Why didn't you speak?"
"There were so many people there I couldn't make my way
through the crowd. I tried to get your attention."
"I didn't know you knew Black."
"You know everybody in Atlanta knew Black."
"You're right."
"How did you know him?"Stunna asked.
"He used to talk to one of my girlfriends."
"Lani?"
"Yeah," Starr said.
"I knew Lani and I know Jada. As a matter of fact, Jada told me
how to find you."
Starr looked surprised. "I would have never known."
"I mean, we weren't besties, but we crossed paths in the clubs a
time or two, you know? Damn! This place is crazy. This is like shit
I've only seen on HGTV."
"I'm sure you could afford this. Don't be so amazed."
"It's not a matter of being able to afford something. It's a matter
of having good taste and you have good taste, Starr. This is what I
always admired about you. You came from the same place as we
did, but you always wanted more. Even more than your sister. No
offense, but Meeka is just like me with that hood mentality."
She laughed and said, "So what are you doing with yourself
nowadays?"
He laughed and said, "You know me, Starr."
"Well, let me tell you this, my friend. That life is not going to last
always."
He smiled and there were butterflies in her stomach.

Stunna avoided her eyes and said, "Look, I am who I am. I don't plan on changing for nobody."He paused."I play the hand I was dealt."

"There is so much more to life than hood shit."

His eyebrow's raised "Is there really?"

"I know you made your money."

"You know that?"

"The last time I saw you in front of Lennox a few years ago, you were driving a yellow Lamborghini."

He looked confused, like he was trying to remember the day.

"How is your sister?"

"You mean my brother?"

"That's not nice."She laughed.

"I love that girl to death. Still trying to sleep with every woman in the A."

"Just like her big brother."

He grinned and said, "What do I have to do with this?"

"You know I've heard that you're a ladies man."

"If I can find the right one."

"I've heard that before."

"Can we hang out sometime?"

"I have to tell you something," Starr said.

"What?"

"I have a son."

"What? How old?"

"He's about to be seven. He's not my biological son. My ex-boyfriend Trey got killed and I adopted his son."

"Oh, I don't care if he was your biological son or not. I'll take the whole package."His eyes did a once-over her body. "Goddamn! You look fucking amazing."

Those smile lines remerged.

"Do you work out?"he asked.

"I hate exercise."

"And you don't need to start. My Gawd!"

"Boy, would you stop looking at my body like a creep," she laughed.

He licked his lips then he said, "My bad."He turned his gaze "So how is business?"

"It's good right now."
A long pause. He tried his best not to look at her in a creepy way.
"How many kids do you have?"
"Three in all but my oldest is seventeen."
"Are the two youngest by the same woman."
"Different baby mamas."
"Yeah."He removed a phone and presented her with a photo of a little boy and a girl sitting on a wagon. They resembled each other and were almost the same size. "My heart. I love them so much. This why I do what I do."
Starr shot him a condescending smile. "Really? Is that why you do what you do?"
"Well, part of the reason I do what I do."
Starr kept staring at the picture. "I thought you said the two youngest had different mothers?"
"I do, I wanted them to take pictures together. I think it is important for them to know each other."
"They look like twins. What are their ages?"
"Three."
"Who is three?"
"Both of them. They were born a month a part."
"What the hell? You had two women pregnant at the same time?"
"I didn't mean it to happen."
Starr passed him the phone and said, "That is just trifling behavior."
"I didn't mean for it to happen like that."
"But it did."
"You need to get one of your own," he said. "You know, a biological one?"He smiled and said, "I can help you with that."
"Whoa. Slow down, man. I'm not looking for a sperm donor. I need a man. Well, let me rephrase that. I want a man. And I resent that biological statement. I love my son just as much or more than you love your kids."
"I didn't mean it like that."
"I know."
"You don't need a man, but you want a man?"
"Yes."
"So, here I am."

"Slow down."
"So you haven't been with anyone since Trey?"
"I have."
"Do I know him?"
"No, you don't know him. I don't even want to talk about him."
"I'd rather talk about you and me."
"Stunna, you're in the drug game."
"I am. Is that a problem?"
"It is."
"Why?"
"It's selfish. What about your children? If you get killed, what will happen to them?"
"They'll be good."
"What do you mean, they will be good? You think Black's kids are good? Two of them got murdered and the rest of them are left without a father."
Stunna licked his lips and this sent chills down Starr's body. She wanted him physically.
"Look, Starr, I know you think I'm some uneducated hood dude that don't think, but actually, I'm pretty smart. I have a trust fund for my kids. I have bought land down in Newnan, Georgia. Lots of land. So if I get murdered. They'll be good."
"Monetarily maybe, but there are some things money can't buy."
"Like what?"
"Like your life back. Look at Black and all the kids he left behind."
Stunna wasn't trying to hear all that preaching. He loved the game and he had no plans to get out.
"Well, just let me take you out—me, you, and the kids. Your son and my kids."
"You trying to get at me through my son?"
"Maybe."
"Smart man."
"Beautiful woman."
She blushed.
"So are we going out?"
"When?"
"You tell me."
"Next weekend."

"We can take the kids out. Get some ice cream or something."
There was a long pause before she finally said, "I'd like that."

***

Jada and Shantelle sat on her balcony, drinking peach smoothies when Jada's doorbell rang. Jada sprang from her seat and bee lined to the door. She looked through the peephole and saw Fresh. She invited him in. He didn't look the same. His clothes were dingy and his long, wavy hair was unkempt. Beard stubble blanketed his face. He was still a very gorgeous man, but she wasn't used to this cave man presentation.

"What are you doing?"he asked.
"Drinking smoothies with my girlfriend. Do you want one?"
"Can we talk?"
"We're talking. She's outside."She could tell something was troubling him. "Where you been?"
"In Houston for a few months laying low."
"You couldn't call?"
"I didn't call anyone. Not even Q."
"You haven't talked to Q?"
"No, I went to his building. They said he wasn't there and they didn't know when he would be back. They were acting all weird and shit."
"He was arrested for conspiracy to commit murder."
"What?"
"Yeah. They locked him up for Trey's murder."
"What?"
"Yeah."
"Damn."
"So you haven't heard? There has been a lot of shit going on since you were gone."
"Like what?"
"Black is dead."
"What do you mean, dead? How did he die?"
"He was murdered."

"Please tell me you're lying."

"No. I'm not. I wish I were."Jada's eyes were misty.

"Damn. What happened?"

"Nobody knows. Some people think it was some Detroit niggas. Some say it was dudes out of California. His body was found on the side of Roosevelt Highway in College Park. What did you want to tell me?"

"I'm running."

Jada's eyebrow's squished together. "Running?"

"On the run. On the lam."He paced.

"Oh my God! For what?"

"Double murder."

"Double murder? You're kidding, right?"She scanned his face but his eyes were telling and she knew that this was not a joke.

"It's a long, complicated story, but the short version of it is I copped some work and some dudes tried to take me out. They killed my homeboy and they were going to kill me. I got them before they got me."

"Damn."

He paced and stopped and turned to her. "Nobody is to know about this, Jada."

"Why did you tell me?"

"I trust you."

"This case sounds like it is self-defense. Why don't you just turn yourself in?"

"It is self-defense. But you don't know what it's like in Texas. I ain't exactly got the best record, Jada. I can't go down for two murders. I'll never get out."

"So, you need my help?"

"If you can. If you can't, I'll understand."

"What do you want me to do?"

"I need you to get in touch with this Mexican named Gordo. He's in Houston. I'm going to buy you a ticket. I want you to go down there and I'm going to give you the address of a restaurant. Leave word there for Gordo to call me."

"Why didn't you do it when you were in Houston?"

"When I tell you I was laying low, I was laying low. I was actually at my grandma's house out in Port Arthur, which is an hour away.

There was no way she was going to do that shit for me. It was me and her and I didn't think I would need to find Gordo. I thought Q would help me, but he's not here, is he?"
"Yeah, you're right."
"I need Gordo's help. I need to make some bread. I'm going to need a dream-team defense team. I have two bodies. I'm turning myself in Jada. I know I can't run forever. Somebody saw this and PoPo is probably looking for me, but meanwhile, it takes money to live."
She hugged him and she thought about the time Shamari was on the run.
"Fresh, I know you have money for an attorney."
"I do, but I don't know what my bond is going to be. Or if I'm going to even get a bond. And I want a defense team, not just one lawyer, and that's going to cost hundreds of thousands of dollars."He paused. He said, "I love you, Jada."
"I love you, too."
"You still with that Tank dude?"
"No. But my ex got out."
"What do you mean, he got out? How did he get out?"
"Informant recanted his statement."
"So damn! You're going to get back with him?"
"No, we're friends. He's my best friend and you'll have to understand that. And he's going to understand about you."
"What about me?"
"I was just telling Starr the other day that I wished it could have worked with us."
"I want it, too."
"Are you saying that because you're going to jail?"
"No. I thought about that when I visited you and that clown-ass Miami dude was over here."
She kissed him just as Shantelle burst through the door. Jada introduced Fresh to Shantelle.
"Damn. You look familiar, shorty." Fresh said.
Shantelle looked surprised. She knew who he was, too. She didn't know his name, but she'd seen him a few times with Q when she made pickups for Trey.
"Yeah, you were a runner for Trey, right?"Fresh said.

"You knew Trey?"
"I did, but not well. I'm from Houston."
She smiled. "I've been down there a time or two."
He kissed Jada and said, "I've got to be going."

Later that night, Shamari came over to watch NARCOS on Netflix with Jada. Though she had seen all of the episodes, she was happy to be doing this with him. She was happy that he was out. Midway through a show, his hand crawled up her thigh. Though she had fucked him once since he had been out, she didn't want to lead him on. She didn't see him like that. Truth was that she hadn't seen him like that in a long time. Even before he had gone away. She would always love him, but there was no need for them to do something that she would regret. Sure she fucked men for fun, but she did have feelings for Shamari and she knew those feelings could easily get mistaken for love.

"What's wrong, Jada?"

"I don't want to do what we're going to regret."

"But you're my woman."

She sat up on the sofa and said, "Mari, I'm not your woman. You know I love you but the truth is that we wasn't on great terms before you left."

"Why, Jada? Why don't you want me?"

"I can't explain."

"What's wrong with me?"

"Nothing is wrong with you. You just don't do it for me anymore." Hearing her say this infuriated him. How in the hell could she say he didn't do it for her? He had been there for her and with her for years and now she was saying that he wasn't doing it for her?

"That's bullshit and you know it, Jada. Just tell me. You still with that dude that you were fucking with when I was inside?"

"I'm not with anybody."

"When was the last time you saw him?"

Silence.

He laughed. "So you're not going to answer the question?"

"I was with him today."

“You fucked him?”

“No, but if I did, it’s my business.”

“You probably did.”

“Look, Mari. You need to leave. Get the fuck out of my house right now.”She marched right over to the door and opened it. “Get out!”

“I ain’t going.”

She huffed. “What’s wrong?”

He said, “Look, I’m sorry, Jada. The whole time I was inside, I couldn’t wait to get out because I thought there was a chance for me and you. I thought you would be happy that I was out and we could make some babies. I don’t know. I was just dreaming, I guess.”He laughed, not because anything was funny. He was dying inside.

“I’m sorry. I know how hard this must be for you.”

“You’ve been trying to tell me. I get it.”

“Good. Look, whatever you need me to do, I’ll do. You know I’ll always be here for you, but just not in that way.”

“I got you. Hey, how can I get mad when you are keeping it real with me?”

 She held the door as he strolled toward the exit. He stopped and said, “Jada, there was an FBI agent that came to my sister’s house the other day.”

“What?”

“He said he used to work with Black. He said that they were partners. Do you know anything about that?”

“TeTe was just talking about that today. She said that this guy was taking drugs from drug busts and splitting the profit with Black.”

“So that’s where he probably got the money to give me.”

“Yeah. I think, but I don’t know.”

“What did he want?”Jada asked.

“Wants to partner up with me.”

“What?”

“I don’t want no part of that guy.”

“That’s right. So what are you going to do?”

“I don’t know. Sooner or later, I’m going to have to get off my ass though.”

“I’m sure.”

She hugged him. He squeezed her ass and she slapped his hand.

***

The girl named Ava that Jada had met at the gym had DM'd Jada about sixteen times before Jada finally decided to meet up with her for lunch and cosmopolitans at Joy Cafe in Buckhead. Ava wanted to know where Jada lived and how did she live so fabulous. She also wanted to know where she was employed. She was just getting too damn nosey, so Jada lied to her and told her that she was a high-class escort. Jada hoped that would deter Ava's thirsty ass from sweating her so much, but instead, she wanted to know how much it paid, so Jada had made an arrangement to meet up with TeTe. The three ladies met for dinner and Jada told TeTe that Ava was interested in learning the business.

TeTe looked Ava over. She had a nice body and a gorgeous smile and TeTe asked where she was from.
"I'm from Charlotte, North Carolina."
"A country bitch," TeTe said.
"Excuse me. Atlanta is the country too."
"Sweetheart, don't get offended. I'm from South Carolina. I love being country. It's not where you're from, it's the game that you have."TeTe laughed.
"Where in South Carolina?"
"A little country town called Chester."
Ava said, "My grandmother was from Chester."
"Small world."
"Yup."Ava smiled.
TeTe said, "You ever did something like this before?"
"I've dated men for money."
"This ain't dating, baby. This is hoeing. There is a difference."
"Every woman has sold ass. Maybe not directly, but they've done something sexually for a favor."
TeTe sipped her drink and said, "Exactly."
"How much does it pay?"

"Depends on the client."

"I want the top-of-the-line clients."

TeTe laughed and said, "You see, honey, it doesn't work like that. We don't always get what we want. You're a cute girl and all, but who's to say that the top client might want you. We got some clients that want white bitches, some that want fat bitches, ugly bitches, Hispanic bitches, Mexican bitches."

"Mexican falls under Hispanic" Jada said.

"Who gives a fuck?"TeTe said.

"So how do the clients decide?"Ava asked.

"Your pictures. I'm going to need some pictures to go on the website and if they want you, they will let me know and I'll send you out to meet them."

"What do top clients pay?"

"I just sent a girl to Abu Dubai for fifty thousand."

"What did she have to do?"

"I don't give a damn what she had to do. I got fifty stacks and she got fifty stacks."

"Fifty stacks? What did she have to do? Let somebody shit on her or something?"Jada asked.

"What?"TeTe said.

Jada said to TeTe, "Don't tell me you haven't heard about those thirsty-ass Instagram hotties flying over to Dubai and letting men shit on them for shopping sprees?"

TeTe said, "Oh fuck no. I have established clients. Ain't nobody shitting on nobody unless I do the shitting."

Ava and Jada laughed. Ava liked TeTe. TeTe was funny but she could tell that she meant business. Jada couldn't believe she was sitting here listening to all this.

TeTe said, "So when do you want to start?"

"Now."

"What is your name?"

"Ava."

"I need your full government name. I need to do a background check on you."

Ava and Jada frowned.

"I gotta make sure you ain't been busted for something and trying to bring me down with you."

"Ava. Ava Harrell."
"So what brings you here? Why'd you pick Atlanta?"
"Kind of running from someone."
TeTe's eyebrows rose. "What do you mean, running? Are you running from the law?"
"No, nothing like that. I am running from a crazy man. You know when it was over, he didn't know when to let go."
"He loved you?"
"Yes."
TeTe began to cry and when Jada noticed it, she embraced her. Then Jada removed a Kleenex from her purse and passed it to her. She knew that she was thinking about Black and how much she missed him.
Ava looked confused.
TeTe got herself together and said, "I'm sorry."
"What happened? What did I say?"
"I lost my boyfriend two months ago. I was just thinking about him."
"Sorry to hear that."
"Not your fault."
Ava smiled. "I'm so anxious to start."

***

Starr and Stunna had taken the kids to the Skyzone trampoline park in Roswell. Stunna had only brought his son. His daughter's mother had taken his daughter to Disney World and though T.J. was a few years older than Stunna's son, they bonded. T.J. demonstrated to little Elijah how to play the video games and he liked having him around. Elijah was like T.J.'s little brother that he didn't have. They were jumping on the trampoline and when Elijah leapt off the trampoline, he sprained his arm. He began to cry. T.J. began to cry with him.

Starr said, "T.J., why are you crying? You didn't get hurt."
"I know, but he's just a baby. I don't want him to hurt."
"Aww." Starr rubbed her son's head.

Stunna said, "It's okay, T.J. He's going to be okay. He falls all the time. He's a tough little guy."

Elijah was bawling so loud that people were literally covering their ears. Stunna kneeled and said, "If you don't stop crying, there will be no ice cream for you."

Elijah fought hard to bring his tears to a halt, and they all started laughing.

Later that evening, they ate pizza with the kids. Elijah and T.J. were playing with action figures.

Starr turned to Stunna and said, "Looks like the kids are getting along well."

"They are going to make good step-brothers."

She smiled. "Slow down."

Stunna grinned. He was attractive and charming, and he was masculine. She loved that about him. A man that could handle her. Put her in her place if he needed too. She loved men like that. He seemed sincere.

"So you'd rather get locked up?"Starr asked.

"You know my daddy went to prison. Three of my uncles went to prison. Two of my aunties and my mom did a stint and even me and Micky did a year each. I'm not trying to go back."

"Everybody says that."

"Your point? It's all in my cards. I might make it out. I might not."

"But you can make it out. You can quit right now."

"What if I don't wanna? Why should I?"

"Hey, you're a grown man."

He eyeballed her tiny waist. "And you're a grown-ass woman."

She laughed.

"Let's just enjoy the moment. Let's enjoy each other. You said you didn't want a D-Boy. I respect that. We're having a good time. The kids are having a good time. Let's just leave it at that."

"You're right, sir."

"Besides, what's normal? Name a person that has a normal life. We gotta look at TV to see this picture-perfect shit."

TeTe had received a call from a long-time customer Lanny Michaels. Lanny's job was to be a liaison for famous people that wanted to spend time with high-class escorts and wished to remain anonymous.

"Lanny, where have you been?"
"Month long vacation to Europe. Me and the missus."
"Sounds nice."
"So what you got for me?"
"The question is what you got for me?"TeTe said.
"I have a high-profile client that wants some company from one of your beautiful girls. One of those deals where the girl shows up at the room and only then will she know who he is. He doesn't want cell phones or nothing like that. This shit has to be totally discreet. He wants one girl."
"What is his preferences, black, white, Asian, Hispanic? Short, tall, medium build, lots of ass, no ass, wide hips?"
"He's an athlete so he wants them to be in shape but still feminine, you know what I mean? The kind of woman that goes to the gym but doesn't live at the gym."
"Toned in the right places?"
"Yeah."
"What ethnicity?"
"Doesn't care."
"What? Athletes like exotic. Usually they don't want black girls."
"He loves black girls. He's black."
"That's a damn first."
Lanny laughed and said, "Quit generalizing people. Everybody is not alike."
"You're right. Okay. Have you been to the site?"
"I have. There are some new girls on there. I like that black girl Ava. I think he would like her as well."
"She is a cutie. He would be her first."
"Cool."

"What's his budget?"
"Thirty thousand for three nights."
"Okay, I will see if I can work that out. Where is she going?"
Lanny laughed and then said, "I'll send you the information."

***

Jada had traveled to Houston and followed Fresh's instructions. She left word with Diego's sister at Anna's restaurant for Gordo to call him. Three days after Jada returned, Fresh received a call from Gordo, and by the end of the week, Gordo was in Atlanta. They all sat in Jada's living room drinking Absolut vodka and eating salsa chips.

Gordo said, "What happened to Q?"
"I'll let him tell you. I don't exactly know."
"Have you been to see him?"
"No."
Gordo's nose wrinkled "That is supposed to be your friend."
"He is my friend."
"I don't understand then. You don't go see him and he want to keep…"He paused.
Fresh wondered what he was trying to say. He knew Gordo had trouble with translation sometimes.
"He tries to keep what?"asked Fresh.
"Secret."
"What kind of secret?"
"We were going to kill Diego."
"Who was going to kill Diego?"
"Me and Q."
"Really?"
"Yes. The plan was to get Q to make a deal with him and then I was going to send my team in to take him out."
"Your own cousin?"
"Yes. You and Q are like family to me, but I'm wondering, are you like family to each other because you never knew this?"
This was shocking to Fresh. He wondered why Q never told him. Then he wondered why Diego stopped dealing with him toward

31

the end of his life. Perhaps he sensed something. Or perhaps Q told him to stop dealing with him. Shady motherfuckin' character.

"Look, that's why I wanted you to come visit. I didn't want to say too much over the phone, but I'm wanted for murder. I killed two people in Houston."

Gordo narrowed his eyes.

"They were trying to rob me."

"I understand."

"I need help."

"We need each other."

Fresh sipped his drink and said, "I need a shipment."

Gordo cut his eyes at Jada. He never liked discussing business in front of women.

Fresh said, "She's cool. She's my girlfriend. Soon to be my wife."

Jada smiled. She knew it was all bullshit. Maybe it wasn't, but why did he get this epiphany now that he was on his way to jail, perhaps prison.

Jada stood. "I'll just go to my room and catch up on HOUSE OF CARDS."

After she disappeared, Gordo said, "So, what happens if you get locked up and you aren't able to pay me the money?"

"That won't happen."

"The Policia is after you?"

"They are."

"So you don't know if it will happen or not."

"You're right. I can't promise you that, but anytime you consign someone something, there is always a risk involved."

"True."

Fresh said, "Look, man, I need you more than ever. Remember, I convinced Q to see you when he didn't want to see you. Now, there is no Q and no Diego."

"What happens when they catch you?"

"I'm going to beat this case. I'm not going to run. I'm turning myself in."

"And after you beat it?"

"We can go right back to work. I'm going to hustle till I die. This is all I have."

"And it's all I have, too."Gordo downed the liquor, then stood and made his way to the door.

When the door closed, Jada appeared and said, "Fresh, tell me the goddamned truth. Did Q have something to do with Trey's murder?"

Fresh shrugged. "I know you probably won't believe me but I don't know."

"I believe you."

"Can we talk about something else?"he asked.

Her heart raced and she grabbed his head and kissed him. "So, I'm going to be your wife?"

"If you want to be."

"Fresh, don't bullshit me. You know every girl wants to be a wife and I don't appreciate you saying that shit just because you are going away."

"I'm saying this because I'm growing up, Jada. I see a woman I want to be with and I need to get her."

"I want you to meet my mom."

"After I surrender, I'll meet the whole family."

"I have a sister that I want you to meet, too. She gets high. She is in and out of rehab. I don't see her that much and I have a stepbrother that is in prison. Well, not a stepbrother, but a half-brother. We have the same father but not the same mother."

"I want to meet them all. Let me take care of this. I want to make some money and beat this case and settle down."Then he looked at her with serious eyes. "I'm not getting out of the game. This is what I do. This is what I'm good at."

"I understand."Of course Jada would want her man to get out of the game but she had come to terms that this was her fate.

"Now, I need somebody to help me get rid of this shit that I got coming. You think Shamari would help?"

"You can't be serious?"

"I am. Black said he was a good dude."Jada studied his face and realized that he was.

"I'll ask."

***

Jada stood in front of him in a black bodysuit. Shamari imagined her fucking Fresh. Sucking Fresh. Getting doggy styled by Fresh. And she had the nerve to ask him to help Fresh? The man that was fucking the woman that he loved. Shamari laughed when Jada asked him to help Fresh get rid of his product. "You can't be serious?"

"He asked me to ask."
"You love this man?"
She was silent. She knew that if she answered the question truthfully that it would hurt him.
"I know you do."Shamari said.
"Do you wanna help or not?"
"I just got out. Did you forget about that?"
"I know."
"You want me back in prison?"
"Of course I don't."
"Between you and this punk-ass FBI agent, y'all are determined to put me back in the drug business."
"I think Fresh wanted me to ask you just because you are from Atlanta."
"And so are you."
"Hey, he asked me to ask and I asked."
He stood there contemplating, He had no solid plan for making money. He had the funds that Black had left him and he had wanted to help Black's remaining kids any way that he could. He said, "What's in it for me and why is this dude so desperate to recruit me?"
"Because you're real, Shamari."She paused and said, "They're not too many real dudes out here."
"There are lots of real dudes out here, Jada."
"Not like you. They don't build them like you, Mari."
"Whatever."
"Can you help?"
"Is it important to you?"
"It is."

He laughed and said, "Jada, Jada, Jada. The dope boy's best friend."

Jada slapped the fuck out of him. "So what are you saying, Mari?"

"I'm just saying you can't keep living your life like this. Starr has found her a way to stay away from the D-Boy lifestyle."

"Did she?"

"Well, at least she is trying."

"I'm not Starr."

"I understand."

"You in or not?"

"What's in it for me?"

"Low prices."

"What do you call low prices?"

"He told me to tell you if you partner up with him, you can get a block for sixteen thousand."

Damn, Shamari thought. He had never had a price like that in Atlanta. He could make a few moves and then do something else. "I'm in, but this dude better not be a clown."

Gordo had agreed to do business with Fresh, but they would start small because his uncle had just lost a thousand kilos when Diego was murdered. His uncle was suspicious since Fresh was one of the last people that Diego saw before he was murdered.

Fresh needed someone to bring the product back and Shantelle seemed like the perfect fit. She had transported for Trey, so she knew the routes from Houston to Atlanta. She said that she would agree to do it only if Q didn't know about it and Fresh had assured her that he wouldn't find out. Three weeks later, she had brought the product back. Fresh and Shamari worked well and got along even though he was Jada's ex. After a month passed, Fresh invited Shamari to his home and poured him a glass of apple Ciroc. Fresh passed Shamari the shot of Ciroc and they sat in the living room. As they watched THE PEOPLE VS. OJ SIMPSON, Fresh said, "You know, Shamari. I like you a lot, man, and you seem a lot cooler than Black. I liked Black a lot. He showed me a lot about Atlanta, but Black only traveled in the fast lane, you know with him it was trap all night and chasing strippers and baby mama drama and I knew he was dealing with some crazy older bitch named TeTe. Black brought a lot of baggage."
"I know what you mean."
Fresh strolled to the other side of the room where there was a bag of weed on a table.
He looked at Shamari. "Mind if I smoke?"
"I could care less."
Fresh lit the Swisher, took a toke, and said, "Do you smoke?"
"I used too."
"Look, I think I need to tell you something that Jada may or may not have told you."
Shamari's eyebrow's squished together. "What?"
Fresh inhaled and coughed. Then coughed again. Then coughed again. He was smoking some powerful shit indeed. "First, I wanted

to say I'm sorry how this whole thing went down with Jada and all.
I mean, getting to know you really fucks with me. I didn't know
how cool you were. Had I known you before, this would have
never happened."
"You wouldn't have fucked my girl?"
"I love her."He inhaled the Swisher. "I'm sorry."
"No need to be. She's not my girl. I cared about her. I wanted to
be with her, but she made it clear that she didn't want to fuck
with me, so I had to move on."
"Yeah."
"And you didn't do anything that she didn't allow you to do."
"Right."
Fresh sat back across from Shamari. He took possession of the
remote and powered down the TV. He then deaded the swisher.
"I'm on the run, bruh."
Shamari narrowed his eyes. Was he serious?
"Yeah. I thought it was best that I tell you."
"On the run from what? Who?"
"I'm wanted in Houston. I murdered two dudes that were going to
kill me."
Shamari lips parted then he gasped.
"I guess Jada didn't tell you?"
"She didn't. What the fuck?"
"I told her not to say anything."
"Did she tell you about my situation?"
"She told me that you just got out."
"Exactly! which is why she could have at least told me."
"I told her not too. I'm sorry."
Shamari stood and strolled. Fresh cut him off. He stood in front of
him and said, "Look, if it makes you feel any better, I want you to
know I'm surrendering in a few weeks and I'll let you meet the
connect."
Shamari raised his eyebrows and said, "Why would you do that?"
"I like you."
Shamari didn't know whether he liked Fresh or not, but he did
respect him for telling him that he was on the lam. He didn't have
to tell him shit.
"Let me think about it."

As Shamari left, Shantelle entered. She greeted him but he said nothing.
"What was his problem?"she asked.
Fresh said, "I don't know. He's just having a bad day."

***

Dressed in a white backless dress that she'd ordered from Hot Miami Styles Ava pranced around the penthouse suite of the Four Seasons hotel like she was a queen. She was wondering who this high-profile client was. Though a lot of people probably would look down on her for her occupation choice, it was a means to an end. And she had to leave Charlotte. There were people that wanted her dead.

She thought back to the day that she and her best friend, Shakira, and her boyfriend took the money from a drug lord that had trusted her. She knew that if Mario ever found her, she would be dead. She knew that they were still looking for her. A few months ago, she had posted a picture on Instagram of her and her sugar daddy, George, on the island of Santorini, and someone had commented that she was going to be a dead bitch. She had to make money so she could buy her a dream home and the nightclub she always wanted and hopefully meet a nice man that didn't know about her past. But she had to act fast.
She was elated that TeTe had decided that she could work for her. She had created a profile on those sugar daddy websites, and while it was effortless to get a man to splurge on her, they usually demanded a relationship and she didn't want to fuck with those old, shriveled up, white men night after night. Working as a high-class escort was much easier. She had told TeTe that she desired athletes and dope boys, and if she had to go out of the country, she would travel to Abu Dhabi or Dubai.
She would just get wasted, fuck the client and be on her way. There would be no hanging around, cuddling, toying with his old sagging balls smothered with gray pubic hair. Yuck! She wanted to puke just thinking about it. She strolled over to the curtain and peered into the Atlanta night then checked her watch. It was 7:44

p.m. Where the hell was the client? He was fourteen minutes late. She grabbed a bottle of Coke from the fridge. As she was about to open the bottle, the door opened and there he was—the client. A tall, gorgeous, black man with lustrous chocolate skin and sparkling white teeth. He was wearing a black Nike running suit and a pair of black Nike Huaraches.

He closed the door then secured it with the gold chain attached to the door, and turned and said "Hi."

She stood and she recognized him right away—DeSean Cummings, the quarterback for the Atlanta Falcons. What the fuck was he doing here? Why was he buying pussy? Wasn't he married? But it wasn't her job to ask questions. She just smiled and said, "I'm Ava."

"I'm—."

"I know who you are."

He made direct eye contact with her. "You have to keep this under wraps."

"No problem. It's my job."

He plopped on the bed and clasped his hands behind his head. "I bet you're wondering why I'm here."

She smiled and said, "Not my place to wonder."

He said, "You're even more beautiful in person than you are on the pictures."

"Thank you."She blushed. She couldn't believe it and she wanted to smile harder. She couldn't believe that this multi- millionaire athlete was right here in her hotel room, telling her how great she looked.

He said, "Why are you doing this?"

"Huh?"

"You know, like selling your body?"He crossed his arms.

She shrugged her shoulders and said, "I dunno."Though she knew exactly why she was selling her body.

"I'm sure you could easily get a man to take care of you."

She took a swig from her Coke and said, "You don't look like the type that needs to buy pussy either."

He laughed and said, "So you don't drink?"

"I do."

"What's up with the Coke?"

"I was waiting on you to get here and I guess I got thirsty."
"Let's order some drinks."
"What do you want?"
"Surprise me."
"I can go to the liquor store if you want. It's cheaper."
"No, just order it from the bar. I really don't need anyone knowing I'm here."
"I can go. You can stay here. I won't tell anyone."
"Look, just order from room service. Don't worry about the cost."
"Oh, excuse me, Mr. One-Hundred-Million-Dollar Man."
"I didn't mean it like that."
"How did you get in here without someone recognizing you?"
"The freight elevator."
"When was the last time you were here.?"
"Not in a while."
 She called downstairs and ordered a bottle of Hennessy and a bottle of Patron. The liquor was delivered fifteen minutes later. After two drinks, they were both relaxed. She was lying on the bed next to him, massaging his chest, and he asked, "Do you smoke?"
"Weed?"
"Yeah."
"Sometimes. You got any?"
He stood up and dug into his pocket. She lusted at his traps and his broad shoulders. She would have bet a million dollars there was an eight pack under his shirt. Greek God status for sure. She would have fucked him for free, but it would have to be another time. Right now she was here on business.
He removed the Sour Diesel—pungent, frosty, light green buds that lit the whole room up.
She said, "Don't you get tested?"
"Tested?"
"For like drugs and stuff?"
"The season is over, but yeah sometimes they test us randomly. I'm not worried though. I know how to pass the test."
"You want to throw all that money away taking a chance of being labeled as an addict?"

He smiled and licked those beautiful ripe lips. She wanted to rip that goddamned Nike suit off his lean body. She wanted that man inside her.

"That's about the only thing they haven't said about me this season."

"Huh?"

"Do you even watch football?"

"No."

"Well, how do you know me?"

"Nike and Gatorade commercials."

"I had one of the worst years of my career. Statistically, I was the worst in every quarterback category so you won't be seeing me on any commercials anytime soon."He sighed then dumped those frosty buds into a cigar, before rolling a blunt.

"You're depressed."

"I'm not depressed."

"I think you are."

He looked annoyed and then said, "Well, if that's what you want to call it."

"You have a lot to be thankful for."

"Do I? Like what? Besides having money and having to take care of every goddamned soul in my family. Not including my friends. This shit is a curse."

"What about your God-given abilities. You know how many people would kill to be in your position. You're a starting quarterback in the NFL!"

"Let me tell you about God-given abilities. Especially when it came to me. I never had any. I was the clumsiest kid on my Pop Warner football team. I couldn't even throw. The kids in my neighborhood said I threw like a girl, so I was determined to be the best. I practiced my ass off, throwing four hours a day. So do I believe in God? Yes. But I worked for everything that I have."

"So what happened this season?"

"I lost focus. I started believing the hype."

"But you can work to get back to the top."

He laughed and said, "I don't know about that."

"Why not?"

"Rumor has it that I'm going to get traded."

He lit the blunt, inhaled it, and then passed it to her. He sat back down beside her and she stroked his shoulders. He told her all of his problems from having two kids by two different women. There was a third one on the way by a stripper that he didn't even remember having sex with. How he had grown up in a single-parent household, and they were so poor, they didn't have toilet paper. His mother, who worked at McDonald's, would have to steal napkins, so they could wipe their asses. She felt bad for him when he finished telling her his life story. They were both in tears. He paid her and even gave her a bonus even though there was no sex. He vowed that he would call and a week later, he did. They met at the same place, at the same time. He was dressed the same way. He wore a Nike sweat suit, but this time, he had white Nike Huaraches. This time, he asked her if she could get him coke.
"Soda?"
"No."
"White stuff?"
"Yes."
"For who?"
"Me."
"You don't need to do that."
"And you don't need to do what you're doing."
"What am I doing?"
"Selling ass."
"Well, that's what I thought I was doing."
"Can you get it or not?"
"I don't know. Let me call around."She called TeTe who answered the phone on the first ring.
"Hello?"
"I'm with the football player and he wants drugs."
"Weed?"
"White girl."
"I'm not a drug dealer, but whatever you gotta do to make him happy, you do it."TeTe hung the phone up and Ava didn't know who else to call.
Seconds later, TeTe called and said, "Call Jada. Her man is a trapper. Call her and tell her what you need."
She called Jada.

"Can you help me?"
"What's up?"
"I need some white girl."
Jada stared at the phone thinking, I know this country-ass bitch
didn't ask for drugs on my phone. "What are you talking about?"
"It is for a client."
Jada cut her off. "Where are you?"
"The Four Seasons."
"Meet me in the lobby in an hour."
An hour later, Jada was snapchatting in the lobby of the Four
Season's hotel. Her snapchat was captioned: DOING BOSS SHIT AT
THE FOUR SEASON'S HOTEL. Her followers didn't need to know that
she wasn't really staying at the Four Seasons and they damn sure
didn't need to know what she was really there for. Ava spotted
her and walked over during one of her self-indulgent snaps.
Jada turned the camera to Ava and said, "Ava, say hi to my
followers."
Ava smiled for the camera and said hi. After the Snapchat session
was over. Jada passed Ava the coke and she handed Jada the
money.
Ava said, "Thanks."
"No problem."
"It's not for me."
"I don't care."
"But really it's not."
"Okay."
"Do me a favor?"
"What?"
"Don't tell anyone."
"Who would I tell?"
Ava smiled and said, "Right."

***

Later that night, Ava was lying on the bed, wearing a black
leotard, as DeSean sat in a tiny, contemporary, plastic yellow
desk across the room and snorted lines of coke. He was
completely oblivious to her.

43

She crawled to the edge of the bed. "I don't understand. Why are you doing this to yourself?"
He turned to her and said, "You'll never understand."
"You're feeling sorry for yourself?"
He screamed at her and said, "It's either do this coke or die."
"Is life that bad?"
"I've been successful at everything-especially sports. I was a two-sport All American in high school and an All American in college. I won the Heisman trophy. Without football, I am nothing. Nobody cares about me when I'm not performing at a high level. This is not what she signed up for, but she was getting paid and getting paid well. He was so high that she knew that he wasn't going to want to have sex. It was clear to her, that this man had some serious issues and she felt very sorry for him.

Stunna brought Starr to his Grandma Noni's house. Noni was sixty-eight and she had birthed six boys and three girls. All but two of them, were all hustlers. One of her daughters had gone to medical school and was a doctor. Her youngest son had turned out to be an addict. Every Sunday the family met at Noni's house for dinner. Today, Stunna brought Starr over. Stunna's sister Micky was there, looking just like a teenage boy. She had two girls, Goldie and Kelsey, beside her. 'Her bitches' as she called them. They looked amazing, like video vixens. Both were five foot seven and curvy. Micky, being only five foot three, appeared very odd with them. She hugged Starr when Starr entered the house. Then Micky stepped back and examined Starr's body.

"Fine ass, Starrlito."
Starr said, "Don't start with me, Micky. You know we don't get down like that."
Micky smiled, revealing diamond-clustered gold teeth. "Hey, can't a girl dream?"
Goldie, one of her stupid-ass girlfriends, just stood there, running her fingers through her blond wig as Micky flirted with Starr.
"You know I'm just kidding."Micky eyeballed her brother. "And I want you to know that you're all he's been talking about lately."
Starr smiled.
"I heard what happened to your ex-boyfriend, Trey. That was some fucked-up shit."
"Yeah."
Micky turned to the girl that was still grinning, and said, "Bae, this is my home-girl Starr. We used to hang out together back when I was a girl."
"You're still a girl."Starr said.
Micky turned to Stunna and said, "Treat Starr right, bruh."
"What are you talking about," Stunna said.

Micky stood, grabbed Starr's hand, and spun her around. "Look at this woman. She likes nice shit," Micky said as she looked at Starr. Starr frowned and said, "I do like nice things, but I can buy nice shit for myself. I don't need a man for that."

Micky said, "So you're the reason bruh been acting all friendly and shit."

"He's always friendly to me."

"That's to you."

Stunna grabbed Starr's hand and led her into the dining room. Twelve other people gathered around the table. Grandma Noni said grace and they ate mac and cheese, potato salad, fried chicken, pot roast, and sweet potato pie. After dinner. Starr thanked Noni for the delicious meal and gave her a hug. Starr stood in the driveway waiting on Stunna who was still in the house.

Micky came out to join her. "Starr, it was good to see you."

"Same here," Starr said.

"Hey, you know I always liked you. You were like the sister I never had."

"I felt the same way."

"I wanted to talk to you about something."

"What?"

"Look, I don't need nothing to happen to my brother."

"What is that supposed to mean?"

Micky smiled and said, "Nothing. I just heard some foul shit about you. Like as soon as Trey got murdered, I heard that you supposedly had something to do with it."

"I don't care what you heard. I would never have anything to do with murdering a man I loved."

"Really now.?"

There was a long silence and Starr wondered how did Micky hear this and whether this was what was being said about her on the streets.

"Nothing better happen to my brother."

Starr said, "Excuse me? How did we go from you're being glad to see me to this?"

"I had a thought."

"And you think I'm going to do something to your brother, or better yet, you think I had the love of my life killed? Girl, bye. I don't have time for this."

"Come on, Starr, you can cut all that bourgeois shit out. You know I know you and you can come in here talking all that fancy talk, but at the end of the day, you're always on the prowl looking for a D-Boy. Somebody with money. You can roll your eyes if you want."

"I'm sorry you took it that way."

"That's the way I took it."She paused then said, "Remember what I said."

"I'm not even seeing your brother like that."

"You're leading him on."

"He's a grown man."

"Well, we both know how pussy can cloud someone's judgement, especially a man's."

"Has it clouded yours?"

"Bitch, please."

"Your brother is a grown man."

"And to me, family is everything. This is what my family is known for and I'm happy with that."

"What are you saying?"

"You might want to stay away from him."

"I'll let him tell me that."

"No, I'm telling you. If you know what's good for you."

"Micky, just like you know me, I know you. And you know damn well you don't want no part of me. I'll still beat the brakes off a bitch ass, you know?"

Stunna appeared and took Starr's arm.

Micky said goodbye, hugged her brother, and told him that she would see him later.

***

Despite the overcast afternoon, Jada and Ava sat on the patio, taking shots of peach Ciroc. Ava said to Jada, "I want to tell you something, but I don't want you to tell anyone."

Jada didn't know anyone she knew. Who would she tell, except TeTe? They had just met. "If you're afraid that I was going to tell anyone, why would you even bring it up?"

"I think I can trust you."

"You don't know me."

"You're right, but you and I are the same."

"What do you mean?"

"The kind of woman that go gets her own."

Jada sipped her Ciroc and said, "Okay."

Though Jada thought Ava was a bit obsessed with her, she did like her and she thought her little country ass was harmless.

"What did you have to tell me?"

"I'm running."

Jada raised her eyebrows. "Running from your ex. Yeah, you told me and TeTe."

"Well, that's not quite right. There are some other dudes after me."

"Dudes. Like who?"

"Well, a few years ago, when I was living in Charlotte. I was fucking with a big-time D-Boy named Mario. I stole a bunch of money from him. I knew that shit was wrong but I was listening to my friends and they convinced me to do it and he's been after me ever since."

"Of course, he would be after your ass. You took money from him."

Ava dropped her head and said, "I know that shit was wrong."

"How much was it?"

"Over a million dollars."

Jada downed all of her drink and said, "You're a dead bitch."

"I know."

"So that's why you came to Atlanta?"

"Yeah."

"This is the wrong place to run to."

"I know, but I don't want to be too far away from home. You know my parents are in Charlotte and that's just right up the road. I can just hit the highway, go up there to see them, and come back home, you know?"

"Yeah, but what about your parents, aren't you worried about them hurting them?"
"Of course, but they don't want to leave. That's the only place they've ever been."
"Why did you tell me?"
"It's been eating at me and I had to tell someone."
"I'm sure."
Ava avoided Jada's eyes.
"I won't tell anyone, but honestly who am I going to tell. I don't know anyone that you know."
"I know you won't."

***

Stunna lived in a luxury townhome in Buckhead. His home was very masculine, decorated in lots of earth tones. He had very basic, brown leather furniture with a huge plasma TV and that was it. Not a hint of creativity. Starr wandered around the home and her mind raced. Since she'd opened her studio, whenever she would visit someone's home, she always wondered how she could make it better. How she could add color. How she could change the energy of the home. How she could "make it pop."She could make his place come alive if he would be open minded and let her. She admired his twelve-foot ceilings.

"I love this place. There is just so much I can do with it."
Stunna said, "Well, I was going to ask you for your expertise."
"I'm here to help."
"I want you to decorate the entire place."
"I will. What's your budget?"
He laughed. "Budget? Stunna don't have budgets."
"Excuse me. Did I offend you?"
"Actually, you did. You put me in the same category as your other male friends."
"Oh my God. Did I hurt your little ego?"
"Can I get you something to snack on or to drink?"

"No. I'm good. Just have a seat, I wanted to talk to you about something that happened the other night at Noni's house."

"Is there something wrong?"His face was concerned.

"You were inside when your sister came outside and pulled me aside. She said to me that she didn't want anything to happen to you."

"What did she mean?"

"My ex, Trey, got murdered by his baby mother and the man I was recently involved with got charged with his death and she is concerned about you."

"I don't need her concern."

"She's your sister."

"I don't need her concern. Don't worry. I will check her on this."

"It's okay, really."

"No, it's not okay. She works for me, not the other way around." Stunna removed his phone and he punched in Micky's number and Starr said, "No, please, don't say nothing to her. I can handle myself."Micky's voicemail came on.

"I don't appreciate this shit. The nerve of that bitch try to confront my lady like that!"

"I'm not your lady and she's not a bitch, she is your sister."

"You're going to be my lady."

"I'm not."

"What's wrong, Starr? I'm not good enough for you?"

"No, it's not that at all."

"Don't tell me you're scared of my sister."

"Hell, no."

She folded her arms. Starr never expected him to pressure so hard to be with him. She guessed it was naive of her to think that he didn't want to be with her.

Jada's hand was inside Fresh's pants, trying to take possession of his member. He extracted her hand and she made a sad face. He stood and fastened his pants.

"Not now, bae," he said.

"What's wrong? Why can't I have none?"Jada pouted. It had been two weeks since they'd had intercourse and she assumed that he had to be fucking someone else.

"Not now," he said.

 She stood and approached him then draped her arms around his waist. "What's wrong?"

When he faced her, his chin quivered and he said, "I murdered two people. Two men that won't see their children grow up. Won't see their parents grow old."

"Your conscience is bothering you."

He sighed and a painful expression covered his face. "It's bothering the fuck out of me. The scene keeps replaying over and over in my head. No matter what I'm doing, my mind always goes back to that day."

"You had to do it. It was either them or you. What about your friend Jabo? You have to think about Jabo. They murdered your friend, Fresh. When you start thinking like that, you have to start thinking about Jabo. His girlfriend. His son. Your son. What if you couldn't see your son?"

"You're right."

"I know I'm right."

Tears welled in Fresh's eyes. "I have to be there for him. I have to be his father too. I have big responsibilities I want to move Jabo's kid's mother here to take care of them."

"What about your own son?"

"I want him to move here too."

"So you don't want to stay in Houston?"

"I love Houston, but I know I can't live there anymore, I gotta get my mind off the murders."

Jada narrowed her eyes. "And your son's mother?"
He laughed. "There is no way I can be with that woman."
"You think she's going to let your son move with you to another state? With another woman?"
"I don't know. But I'm going to try. But I have to be there for my friend's son. I have to. I feel so fucked up right now."He leaned into her and kissed her. "You just have a way of making things seem so much better."
"That's what I'm here for. If you want to talk about it, I'm here. I never really got a chance to ask you the details. Never thought you would open up."
"You're my lady, Jada. I'll tell you anything."
She smiled. She was happy to hear him say that.
He kissed her. "I meant what I said, Jada. I want you to be my wife."
She loved that he said that, but she had been around long enough to know that men would say anything. Especially when faced with the possibility of going to prison.
"We'll see."
"I'm not just talking, Jada."
"Can we talk about something else?"
"Why?"
"I don't want to get my hopes up too high and then get disappointed."
"What makes you think I'll disappoint you?"
"It just doesn't seem right. I've asked you to come meet my mama and you don't want to meet her."
"It's not the right time."
"She won't judge you. She knows the kind of men I like. She knows I don't date good guys."
He laughed and said, "You don't think I'm good?"
"I do, but what I mean is that you're a street nigga."
"I want to get this case behind me and you can start popping out babies."
"Damn! You've done a 360. When I first met you, it was you didn't have time for a relationship and you seemed to be content with one kid."

"You mean a 180." He grinned, " I thought about my legacy. I thought about my son being in this world by himself and it was scary."
She removed his belt and wrestled with him and took possession of his manhood.
He said, "What are you doing?"
She said, "Well, if you're going to be making these babies, you're going to need some practice, sir."
"Is that so?"
She took a knee and he entered her mouth.

***

Ava and Jada sat in the living room watching HOUSE OF CARDS when Shamari arrived with a bag of cash that Jada was to give to Fresh inside a Neiman's shopping bag. He handed over the cash to Jada and he noticed Ava smiling at him and he said, "Who is that?"

"Nobody."
"She's a cutie."
"Trust me, you don't want those problems."
"Hating, Jada Simone?"
"Never."
Ava glanced in his direction. Shamari made his way into the living room area and introduced himself. "I'm Shamari."
"Ava."
Jada interrupted, "My ex."
Ava smiled and said, "Great. I see that y'all are on good terms. I wish I could be like that with my ex."
"Mari is like my best friend."
Ava said, "He's a cutie. You shouldn't have let him go."She winked at Shamari.
Shamari was standing there, smiling and looking stupid as hell. He'd gotten a chance to check Ava's shapely legs out and he wondered about the rest of her body. Did she have curves? What did the ass look like? He wished that she would stand up. She was pretty enough that he knew that he would definitely fuck her.

53

Jada said, "Shamari, we were in here having girl talk. Hit me up later."
Shamari shook Ava's hand again. "Hope to see you again."
 Then he left the house and Jada trailed him outside.
"What the fuck was that all about Shamari?"
"What was what all about?"
"That 'I hope to see you again 'bullshit?"
"You have a man, and I know this girl ain't your bestie. So what's wrong if I fucked with her? I'm single, boo!"He smiled and it irritated the hell out of her.
"It's the principle."
He laughed. "What kind of principle do you have? Your new man and your old man are hustling together."
"That's different."
"Why is it different?"
Jada was quiet. Shamari was right, but there was so much that he didn't know about this girl that she didn't have time to explain.
"Quit blocking, Jada."
"Huh?"
"Ava is grown. She can tell me if she don't want me or not."
"Look, this girl is on the run."
"Like Fresh?"
"No, she's running from D-Boys in North Carolina. She took some money from them."
"I don't believe you."
"Bye, Shamari."
Jada returned to the living room and Ava was still watching HOUSE OF CARDS. She looked up when she saw Jada, "So you and your ex still have a pretty good relationship?"
"Yeah."
"He still buys you things, I see."
"Huh?"
 Ava eyed the Neiman Marcus bag that contained the money for Fresh.
Jada laughed and said, "Well, I was having him take some things back for me and he said he didn't have time."
"Oh."

"Yeah."Jada disappeared into the bedroom and when she returned, Ava said, "I can see he still cares for you."

"Yeah."

"I wouldn't have let him go."

"Do you want to fuck my ex? I saw how you was looking at him."Jada's bluntness startled Ava.

"I would never do that."

"Please, girl! I know your type."Jada laughed.

"Because we're the same."Ava laughed.

Jada picked up the phone and dialed Shamari's number. He answered and she passed Ava the phone.

Ava didn't say anything. She was nervous. She wanted to talk to Shamari, but she was sure that Jada was upset with her. She passed Jada the phone back.

Shamari said, "Hello?"

"Look, I want you to talk to my friend Ava. She's a nice girl. I'm going to text you her number."

"What?"This made absolutely no sense to him. Jada didn't want him to talk to her earlier. What the fuck was going on?

Jada hung the phone up and texted Shamari Ava's number.

***

Shamari arrived at Fresh's place. He needed more coke. Lots more. The product that Fresh had was pure and the streets wanted it. He had connected with some of his old friends including a guy that he had met in prison named Ty. Plus his lazy-ass brother-in-law was making a lot of sales instead of bumming off his sister. At the prices Fresh was giving Shamari, he was able to give it to Hunch for a better price than Hunch could find anywhere in Georgia.

Fresh passed Shamari a suitcase with ten kilos in it. Shamari was about to head out to the car when he said, "Fresh, do you know Ava?"

"No? Who is that?"

"One of Jada's friends, I saw her at Jada's the other day and I was trying to holler but Jada was hating."

Fresh rubbed his chin. "Why?"

"I don't know."

"Don't worry about that. I'll take care of Jada."

Hearing him say that he would take care of Jada kind of pissed him off. Fresh was taking care of the lady that was once his.

"You like her?"asked Fresh.

"That motherfucker is gorgeous."

"Go for it, bruh."

Shamari grinned. "I have her number already. I'm going to hit her up."

"Good for you, homie. Look I have a question for you."

"Yeah?"

"Well, you know about my situation. About me being on the run and shit."

"Yeah."

"I want to go see my homie that's locked up, but I don't have an ID."

"You need a bogus one?"

"Exactly."

"I can get you one."

"Good because I need to see him."

Shamari scrolled through his phone to find Scooter's contact information, Scooter was the guy who had gotten the fake ID for Black that allowed Black to visit him in prison.

The peach-colored Victoria Beckham dress was glued to Ava's body. Shamari marveled at Ava's shapely legs and bubble-shaped ass. Tom Ford heels clacked as the entered Morton's steakhouse. A rail-thin, blond hostess led them to a booth in the back of the restaurant. Ava ordered a glass of Riesling.

"Jada tells me that you're from Charlotte," Shamari said.
"Yeah."
"Never been there."
"It's only four hours away."
"So what's up there besides the Carolina Panthers and your fine ass?"
"I'm here," she giggled.
"That's right. So there is no reason for me to go there."
"My parents are there."She sipped her Riesling "It's an up and coming city. I love it because it's a city with a small town vibe. Very suburban."
"What brings you here?"Shamari wanted to know if she was going to tell him about the people that were after her.
"Change of scenery."
"Running from a bad marriage or something?"
"Running? Why would I be running?"
He laughed and said, "It's just a figure of speech, ma. I didn't mean that you were literally running."He then said. "Are you RUNNING?"
"No."
The waiter dropped the food on the table—two thick porterhouse steaks medium well —hint of pink on the interior, with creamed corn.
 He bit into his steak and she said, "So what about you? Why did you and Jada break up?"
"It was never right from the start. It was more of a brother-and-sister relationship."

She flashed her beautiful teeth. Her smile made his heart skip a
beat.
"But you fucked her. You didn't fuck Tangie, did you?"
"How did you know my sister's name?"
"When you left, you said 'Tangie, I'll be right back. 'I listen."
"You do. Back to Jada. It was never right. But I love her and I'll still
do for her. And vice versa. I met her new man."
"What do you feel about him?"
"He's cool."
"I can't believe she let you get away."
"Let's not talk about Jada. Let's talk about Shamari and Ava."
She smiled again. His dick pulsated. He wanted to rip that dress off
her, and later that night, in a Kroger parking lot, he did exactly
that. He yanked her bra off. She had a handful of tits with
beautiful nipples that stood erect. She stopped his hands from
traveling down to her thighs, tugging at her yellow panties fringed
with lace.
"I can't."
"What do you mean?"
"I don't do one-night stands."
"Who said it was a one-night stand? Hell, you can come pick me
up tomorrow and we can do this all over again."
She laughed.
"What's the problem?"
"I don't want you to leave me."
"I like you, Ava. You know you want me."His hands were now back
between her thighs.
"I do want you."
"What's wrong, babe?"
"Take it slow."
He removed his package from his pants and said, "Jerk me off."
She began to jerk his dick. He was erect and his dick was thick,
juicy, and veiny. The engine was still running. She turned off the
ignition and took him deep inside her mouth. After she gave him
oral, she reclined on the seat and he fingered her until she came.
They climbed into the backseat and he fucked her savagely. He
yanked her hair and he climaxed on her big beautiful ass.

***

Fresh and Q were separated by a glass partition. They stared at each other before Q finally cracked a smile. "I didn't know who you were," Q said.

Fresh had visited under the alias Malcom Boulware. "How you doing?"

"So so."

"Bruh! It's rough out here."

"I called Houston and I heard about what happened."Q spoke of the two murders. They had known each other long enough that they didn't need to speak to understand each other.

"I ain't have no choice," he sighed.

"I understand."

"Do you need me to do anything for you?"

"Have you seen Starr?"

"No."

"Can you go see her for me?"

"And tell her what?"

"Tell her I'm innocent."

Fresh nodded. "Do you need any money?"

"Money is on my books and my attorneys."

"Who is your attorney?"

"I have two."

"Their names?"

"William Hansen and Mike Ferguson."

"Fire them both and get Joey Turch."

"I've heard that name around the jail."

"He's the best. Black swore by him and I've been talking to Shamari and he swears by him too."

"Who?"

"Jada's ex."

"You friends with her ex?"

"No, just working together."

"You said Black swore by him. Past tense."

"Black is gone."

"What do you mean gone?"

"Flat-lined."
"You're lying."Q wondered whether a member of the cartel killed
Black. He remembered that Fresh had thought Black had
something to do with Diego's murder.
Q stared at Fresh and was silent. His eyes asked Fresh whether he
had anything to do with the murder.
Fresh said, "Not on us."
"Good."
Fresh couldn't believe that he said good because the last time
they had spoken of Black, Q had wanted him dead to prove to the
cartel that Fresh didn't kill Diego even though he and Gordo were
plotting to kill Diego."
"Yeah, he's gone."
"Damn."
Fresh looked at the clock behind him, and Q said, "Can you do me
that favor?"
"What?"
"Go see Starr for me?"
"Ok."

***

"There is this dude that my brother-in-law knows from South
Carolina. Wants to buy sixteen kilos, but he wants them in
halves."Shamari said to Fresh.

"Okay, put them in halves for him."
"I can't. I'm staying with my sister and she be tripping and shit. I
can't bring that shit back to her house."
Fresh looked at Shamari side-eyed. "Why don't you have your
own place? You have the money for it."
"You don't know what I've got."
"I know everything. I know that Black left Jada two hundred
thousand dollars for you."
"How do you know that?"he said. "Oh ya, I forgot. You fuckin' my
ex."
 Fresh didn't respond and Shamari resented him.

"Look, can you help me or not? I mean I don't need you. You asked me to help you out."

Fresh knew it was true. He needed Shamari.

"I'll help."

"Good."

"I'm sorry, bruh. I got a lot of shit on my mind."

"I understand and trust me, this shit is aggravating to me too, but this country-ass nigga is buying a lot of weight."

"I got you."

Awkward silence.

"So did you fuck shorty, yet?"Fresh said, trying to lighten the mood.

"I don't kiss and tell."

"So you didn't hit it?"

"I ain't say all that."

"That was fast."

"She's cool."

"You like her?"

Shamari used a red box cutter and ripped into the silver duct tape of the kilo.

"I like her. Seems cool."

Fresh said, "It's funny. I ain't never seen Jada with this girl. You got a picture?"

Shamari removed his phone from his pocket and presented Fresh with the picture.

Fresh studied the picture. Ava was standing in front of a full-length mirror in a purple G-string. "Damn! Baby girl is gorgeous with a banging body."

At one p.m., Jada and Ava sat across from each other in a booth at the back of the restaurant.

"So you fucked him?"Jada asked. She had spoken to Fresh earlier in the day and he had insinuated that Shamari had fucked her. They had had a conversation about her not wanting Shamari to be with Ava because Jada thought that Ava was bad news. Fresh had said that it was too late and she kept asking him what he had meant by that. He never responded so Jada took that as they had had sex.

Jada startled Ava. "I didn't fuck him,"Ava said.

"You're lying."

"Why do I have to lie to you?"

"You don't."

"Why is it your business?"

"It's not my business."Jada sipped her Arnold Palmer. "You move fast."

"And so do you."

"Nobody is after me to kill me."

"That was low," Ava said. Then she paused. "Jada, there is something that you should know about me. I might look cute, but I'll fuck you up."

"I'm damn sure not the bitch to fuck with," Jada said.

Jada dumped a pack of Splenda into her Arnold Palmer. "Look, I'm sorry for what I said."

They locked eyes. "Do you have a problem with me and Shamari seeing each other?"Ava asked. "I mean, you're the one that hooked it up. So, Jada, do you have a problem? I don't know if I could be cool with my ex seeing somebody that I know."

"I'm good."

"So why bring it up?"

"To see would you tell me."

"What did he tell you?"

"He didn't tell me anything."

"Okay, then."
"Look, I just don't want him to get hurt."
"Shamari can handle himself."

***

Inside the grand ballroom of the Hyatt hotel, Stunna held his 34th birthday, sixty guests and a DJ were packed inside. Stunna sat at the head of his table with his two kid's mothers, who were now best friends. Money had that effect on people. He had invited Starr but she declined, she didn't want to be anywhere near Micky. who was there of course with Goldie and Kelsey, 'her bitches'.

Everyone sang happy birthday to Stunna and afterwards they danced. Instead of giving him gifts, Stunna had taken the liberty to get all the guests gifts. He was always generous and always the one with all the flash. Besides, he was the richest man in the room. What could they possibly get him? Inside the gift bags, there were presidential Rolexes.

"This is some real boss shit, right here," Goldie said.

Micky was smiling. "That's how my big brother get down."

"I love it."

Micky nudged her and said, "Don't get too thirsty. You belong to me."

Stunna approached a podium that was now near the front where the DJ was situated. He ordered one of his lieutenants to make sure the door was closed. He stood in the front of the room like he was the CEO of a major company.

He said, "Preciate everyone coming out to turn up with your boy on his born day."

Applause filled the room.

"The watches were my way of thanking everyone who helped me make last year a major success. Last year, we made so much fucking money. And I appreciate y'all."

One of Micky's strippers said, "Your brother is up there talking like what the fuck he is doing is legal."

Micky scowled. "Do you have a problem with it?"

63

"No."
Stunna continued. "This year is going to be even better than last
year. We are going to take over Atlanta. On the count of three, I
want everyone to say, 'Take over the A'."
The chant, "Take over the A", filled the room. Stunna sat back at
the table.
Before they left, Stunna asked Micky to meet him in a private
room away from everyone else.
Micky hugged Stunna and said, "I love you, bruh."
Stunna kissed Micky's forehead and said, "I love you too, but if
you ever disrespect Starr again, I'll slap the fuck out of you.. Don't
ever approach anybody I'm fuckin'with making threats. You ain't
my mama. I can take care of myself."

***

Starr was surprised that Fresh had stopped by her home. They
weren't besties. She invited him in and led him to the kitchen
because T.J. was watching a cartoon, THE SECRET OF KELLS, on
Netflix in the living room area.

"Really nice place."
"I thought you had been here before?"
"If I did, I don't remember. But hey, I smoke. So I don't remember
shit that most people remember."
She laughed and said, "Well, I don't have anything for you to
smoke here, but I can fix you a drink if you want."
"That's okay."
"What's going on? I hear that you and Jada kicking it."
"She's my lady."
"Jada is my ace. I don't know if she told you, but when we first
met, I couldn't stand her and she couldn't stand me. But now, I
love that girl to death."
"I know. This is the right time for me, you know?"
Starr's eyes grew. "The right time because you're on the run?"
"She told you?"
"She tells me everything. Did you not want me to know?"
"I don't care if you know. It's not like you're going to turn me in."

"You're going to turn yourself in, right?"
"I am."
"Good."
"Why is that good?"
"I hear it was self-defense. I think you'll get off."
"I think so too."
"What brings you over?"
Fresh was daydreaming, looking at Starr's succulent lips. He wanted them around his dick. She was a beautiful girl. No wonder Q wanted her so bad. For a moment, he wished they could fuck. Nobody had to know.
"Fresh," Starr said, interrupting his imaginary head job.
"My bad, I was thinking about my case."
"Well it's not a case yet until you have been charged."
"You know a lot about the law."
"Unfortunately, my daddy was a gangsta."
"Mine too."
"Why are you visiting?"
"I saw Q the other day."
"How did you go see Q and you're on the run?"
"Long story. But the short version is I got a fake ID."
"Okay. So, you saw Q?"
"Yes and he told me to tell you that he is innocent."
"And you believe him?"
"I don't know what to believe."
Starr sighed and said, "I do."
"And what do you believe?"
"Q had Trey killed. Look, I don't want to get into all of that. I understand he's your friend and that he wasn't going to say all of that over the jail phones. I mean think about it. Do you think he's going to admit he had someone killed over the phone?"
"True. But how do you know?"
"Just know that I know."
"I ain't here to start trouble."
"Just doing what you're told?"
"I am."
"You seem like a good dude."
"I think so."

"Take care of my girl."
 He stood and was heading out the door before turning around.
He hugged her and said, "Hey, Starr, take care of yourself."
She nodded.

CHAPTER 11

Stunna was surprised when he opened the door and saw his sister standing there looking like a little boy. Her Levis were sagging and she wore an Atlanta Falcon's fitted cap along with a pair of black and white Jordans.

Micky said, "So, are you going to stand there and look at me or are you going to invite me in?"

He stepped back. "No bitches with you today, pimp," he said.

She laughed. "You know how they can be. They can be moody and shit and I can be moody. I'm on my cycle."

That was a little too much information for Stunna. He knew his sister was, in fact, a woman. Got pictures of her with her hair down to her ass and in pink Easter dresses, but when she morphed into a boy, somehow he never thought about her getting a period.

"What's up?"

"I just wanted to say I'm sorry and I love you, bruh."She bumped her chest with her fist and said. "Fo'real, tho'."

"I know you do."

"And I'm sorry for what I said to Starr."

"You let her know that."

"I will."

Micky marched right past him and sat on an ugly green recliner. He sat on a sofa across from her.

"I know you didn't come all the way over here to tell me that you're sorry about what you said to Starr."

"No, not at all."

"Okay, I don't have all day."He glanced at his watch.

"It's about B.C."

"What about him?"

"He just bought a Porsche Cayenne?. I mean, if your trying to take over Atlanta, you might want to do it without him."

Stunna stood and paced. B.C. stood for Byron Cole. He was a UPS driver that Stunna used to get his product from California.

Stunna's connect would send the product to an address provided
by B.C. and B.C. would make sure that the product got to Stunna.
In the last sixth months, B.C. had bought a F150, a white X6 BMW
and now he had bought a Porsche. Stunna knew that it was just a
matter of time before someone noticed that B.C. was living
beyond his means. He would have to pay the man a visit.
"So how do you know this?"
"The other day when you sent me to go see him, he showed up
driving it. I asked him whose it was and he said he just bought it."
"Is that so?"
"Yeah, he said you knew about it."
"He's lying."
"I knew he was."
"I'll take care of it."
"If you want, I can handle it," Micky said.
"No, it's okay. I've told him about this kind of shit before. I'll
handle it."
She stood and was about to walk out the door and Stunna said,
"Micky?"
She turned and faced him. "Yeah?"
"What do you think about Starr?"
"She seems kinda uppity to me now, you know? Like she thinks
her shit don't stank. Her sister Meeka, now. I like that bitch."
Stunna laughed.
"So what do you see in her?"
"Have you ever wanted something different?"
Micky shrugged. "So, what's so different about her? She's just
another hood bitch that thinks she's better than she is. She's fine
and all, but you can have anybody you want."
"I can't have her."
"So, do you think that's what it is? The fact that you can't have
her?"
"Maybe."
"Does she want you to stop?"
"Stop what?"
"Stop dealing."
Stunna looked at her strangely and said, "What made you ask
that?"

"I dunno. She just seems like that type that would want to control a man."

"Nobody tells Stunna what the fuck to do."

***

Byron Cole, better known as B.C., was a twenty-nine-year-old, thin dude with a thin, premature greying mustache. He'd worked for UPS since he graduated high school and it seemed like the ideal job until he and his girlfriend had three boys back to back. The arrival of the kids made it hard for his girlfriend to keep a job. It made more sense for her to stay at home with the children because Byron's UPS salary made it impossible to get a daycare voucher. The UPS salary was good, but it wasn't enough to feed five people and that's where Stunna came in. Stunna had approached Byron and offered a thousand dollars for every shipment of coke that B.C. received and this was more than enough supplemental income. Two years after they had begun, B.C. had fifty thousand dollars in savings. He was able to take care of his kids and his girlfriend and he even got himself a little mistress that he would give a few dollars to every now and then. Life seemed to be great. B.C. still couldn't believe his good fortune. With his keys in his hands and new Yeezys on his feet, he was smiling until Stunna and a big black assed dude named Blue appeared in his sight.

"B.C."

"Stunna."B.C. dropped his keys, he was so startled.

Stunna kneeled and scooped up the keys and handed them to him.

"New car?"

"Yeah, little somethin'."B.C. was grinning hard as hell. Stunna kept staring at him.

"Who is in your house?"

"Nobody."

"Let's go inside."

"Oh."B.C. studied Stunna's face. He was stone-faced; it didn't
reveal anything. Perhaps the reason that they needed to go inside
was to speak.

 B.C. then looked at the Blue standing beside Stunna. The sheer
size of the man's hands made him want to run for the hills. Blue
was Stunna's bodyguard and B.C had heard stories of Blue
smashing dudes head's through glass windows and tossing them
over balconies. He was definitely the wrong dude to fuck with.
Once they were inside, B.C. led them into a den area. As soon as
they entered the room, Stunna slapped the fuck out of B.C. B.C.
slammed into the wall and fell down. He attempted to stand and
then Blue snatched his skinny ass with one hand. B.C. held his
mouth; his front tooth was dangling from his mouth, holding on
for life. The blood sputtered from his mouth.

"Why did you hit me, bruh?"

"Didn't I tell you not to be out here buying a bunch of shit and
putting heat on yourself?"

"Are you talking about the Porsche?"

"You know exactly what the fuck I'm talking about."

Blue released him and B.C. fell to the floor, still nursing his mouth.

"I don't see what the big deal is. You have nice cars. Ferraris and
shit."

"You're not me. You're a punk-ass UPS driver with three kids. How
the fuck can you afford this with your salary?"

"Look, I'm sorry, man."

"Give me the goddamned keys."

"What? I'm not giving you the keys to my car!"

Stunna rushed him and backhanded the shit of him. The tooth was
knocked from his mouth.

"Give me the goddamned key."

"It's in my pocket."

 Blue dug into his pocket.

"I don't see why you handed me the keys back in the first place if
you were going to take them."

Stunna slapped the fuck out of him again and then beelined for
the door.

As they headed out the door, B.C. said, "When do I get my car
back?"

"When I feel like giving it back to you."

***

Jada, dressed in distressed jeans and YSL pumps that she'd just received from Net-A-Porter, stood on Tangie's porch. Shamari attempted to pull her into his arms and steal a kiss, but she resisted. He gripped her ass and she swatted his hand.

"I'm not here for that," she said.
He frowned. "So why are you here and why are you so dressed up? Meeting with the boss man?"
"Huh? What boss man?"
"Fresh."
"Actually, me and Starr are going to get some sushi."
"Is that so? So you decided to stop by to check up on old Shamari?"
"Stop it."
"Why are you here?"
"Did you fuck her?"
"Who?"
"Ava."
"Why? What does it concern you?"
"I'm just asking a question."
"No, you drove all the way across town to ask me some dumb shit."
"Just trying to look out for you."
"What is that supposed to mean?"
"She ain't all what she seems."
"And you are? You should have thought about that before you decided to give your heart to Fresh."
"Stop it, Shamari."
"No, you stop it."
She lusted for his biceps bursting from a light blue V-neck T-shirt.
"Jada, do you love me?"
She avoided his eyes.

He said, "You know nobody knew this and I won't tell anybody, but I'm going to tell you. I almost did some foul shit to Black because I thought you two were fucking around."
She bit her lip.
 He sighed and said, "I almost snitched on Black because I thought y'all were fucking around. But I should have known that Black wouldn't do me like that but you put him in a fucked up position. He wanted to tell me what was going on, but he couldn't."
"I told you. I visited you in prison and I told you that I was fucking with Fresh."
"You did."
"What's the problem?"
"The problem is that you're here on my sister's step and you want to ask me who in the hell I've fucked like you have a right to know."
 Jada said, "You're right, Shamari. I don't have a right to question you."
"Is there something you want to tell me?"
"No."

Fresh entered the jail again under his alias and a jailer brought Q in twenty-five minutes later. The two men tapped hands through the glass.

"What's up?"
"Hired that Joey Turch guy. He's good. We went to court today and he tried to get me a bond and the judge was about to give me a million dollar bond until he realized that I was from Houston. Turch said if I could get someone in Georgia to sign me out, I could come home under house arrest since I have a home here. He didn't want me to spend the million dollars."
"But who is going to sign you out?"
"I don't know. I was thinking that you could get Jada to do it."
"That's out of the question. You know she ain't going to do it. She's loyal to Starr."
"I don't know what to do."
"I'll think of something. I might get Shamari's sister to do it."
"If she can do it. Tell him I'll take care of her nicely."
"I'll ask. That's all we can do right now."
"Right."
"I'm going to try my best."
He needed Q to be out before he turned himself in. One thing for sure is they both didn't need to be behind bars at the same time.

***

Jada and Fresh lay naked in each other's arm after some amazing sex session. His semi-erect penis poked her ass cheeks.

"Have you lost your goddamned mind?"Jada asked Fresh after he asked her to bail Q out of jail. She knew that if she was to go along with Fresh's plan that this kind of betrayal would crush Starr. She laughed and said, "You cannot be serious?"

"I'm just asking."

"Why? Why do you care if Q is out?"

 He said, "Starr is your best friend and regardless what she do, you will be there for her, right?"

"Yeah."

"That's how I feel about Q."

"But I could give two fucks about Q. Look, if Starr don't like the motherfucka', then I don't like him. That's how I roll. I'm not perfect, but I'm loyal."

"I get that."

Jada poured a shot of Patron.

"Do you know anybody who could do this for me?"Fresh asked.

"No."

"Look, I'm not from Georgia. So I'm just asking all the people that I know."

"What about your cousin?"

"He's a square. I know he's not going to do it. That nigga don't want to be involved in nothing illegal."

"Last time I checked, signing somebody out of jail ain't illegal."

"Look, the man is a cornball. He's not going to help."

"I can't help you, partna."

"What about Shamari's sister?"

"Tangie? Hell no! If it ain't got to do with Shamari, she ain't helping, I can tell you right now."

 Why you gotta be so negative?"

"Not negative, just giving you the facts. Look, I love you, Fresh, but I'm never going to cross or hurt my friend intentionally. That's just how I roll."

"I understand. He told me to ask somebody and I did."

***

Jada and Starr were having lunch at Terrace on Peachtree when Starr's phone rang. She didn't recognize the number. She thought it might have been T.J.'s school. At the last moment, she answered the phone.

"Hello?"

"Hey, Starr, this is Micky. Did I catch you at a bad time?"

"I'm at Terrace on Peachtree with my girlfriend."

"Oh. I'm up the street. Mind if I join? I was going to apologize for how I treated you the other night. Since I'm across the street I'd rather say it face to face unless you don't want your girl all up in your business."

Starr said to Jada, "Do you mind if somebody join us?"

"I don't care."

"Look, Micky, you don't have to apologize, but you can come. I know you was just looking out for your brother."

"I want to."

She ended the call and ten minutes later, Micky approached wearing a fitted Atlanta Braves hat, Levis, and Jordans as well as the new Rolex that Stunna had given to her at the party. When she lay eyes on Jada, she said, "Goddamn, mommy. Where the hell have you been all of my life?"

Jada smiled. She'd been known to fuck a girl under the right circumstance but never a girl posing as a guy. Why settle when she could get penetrated by a guy, and this girl looked a hot-assed mess.

Starr introduced the two and Micky sat beside Jada and stared at her erect nipples.

"Who is the lucky man?"

"Fresh."

"From College Park?"

"He's from Texas."

"Damn. Fresh is one lucky-ass dude. I'm sure Fresh can't give you what I can give you."

"Fresh got a tongue too."

Micky laughed and said, "No, you better ask Starr. My brother runs Atlanta."

"Who is your brother?"

"Stunna."

"I know him. Saw him at Black's funeral."

"You knew Black?"

"Yeah."

"I didn't see you at the funeral."

"I was there, but there was thousands of people there. I suppose you couldn't see everybody."

"I would have noticed your sexy ass."Micky licked her lips. "Ma, I can give you the good life."

"I have the good life."

"Don't fuck with girls, huh?"

"Pretty bitches only."

Micky frowned.

"I'm not saying that you aren't pretty but I'm saying girly-girls." Starr interrupted and said, "She was the prettiest girl in my third-grade glass. She had her hair down to her ass."

Micky laughed and said, "In the sixth grade, I realized I liked girls. But Starr is like a sister to me."

Micky turned to Jada and said, "I just like to play around. I hope this Fresh dude makes you happy."

"He does."

Micky turned to Starr and said, "I just wanted to say I'm sorry for the other night."

"I told you that you didn't have to tell me that. We're good."

"I know, but my brother seems happy with you and if he's happy, I'm happy."

Starr smiled and said, "See that's the thing. Your brother and I ain't together. We went out a couple of times but I just got out of a relationship and that's what I was trying to say. What your brother is doing don't have shit to do with me."

Micky said, "I can dig it. I was just saying I know he likes you."

"And I like him, but we are taking it slow."

"Kind of like me and Jada."Micky winked and Jada almost choked on her water.

"You and I are taking it very, very slow, Micky. Like AARP-type slow."

 They all laughed.

Jada's face rested on Fresh's chest. They'd just finished watching a Keeping Up with the Kardashians marathon when he turned to her and kissed her and said, "I think it's time."

"Time for what?"

"Time for me to turn myself in."

"What?"

"Yeah."He sat up on the edge of the bed and she sat up with him and caressed his shoulders.

 She pressed her head against his back. "I don't want you to turn yourself in."

"I can't keep running."He faced her. "There will be no us. There will be no future. No wedding. No kids and I want to see my son."

"So after you turn yourself in?"

"I make bond."

"Then you'll come back to Atlanta?"

"I might get house arrest and I'll have to stay at my mom's house until this is over."

"So you can't come to Atlanta?"

"If I get house arrest, I gotta stay in Texas."

"Then I'm coming to Houston."

"You would do that for me?"

"I would."

He pecked her on the forehead.

"I'm going to beat it."

"I know you're going to beat it if it happened the way you said it happened."

"It happened exactly how I said it happened and both of those dudes had been charged with robberies before."

"So when are you going to turn yourself in?"

"One more run to make."

"Then we're getting married?"

"What?"

"Never mind."

“Talk to me.”

“You’ve been talking all this marriage shit. I guess I was right; it was all talk.”

He sighed and put his hands on his head. “No, baby, it’s not all talk.”

“I want you to meet my mama.”

“I will, but meeting your mom don’t mean shit.”

Jada grimaced. “What do you mean?”

“I didn’t mean it like that. I just meant that meeting your mom will not make me marry you. I have decided that we are going to get married.”

“That’s what you said.”

“You don’t believe me?”

“You’re blowing smoke up my ass.”

“I will if you want me too. I’ll do anything you want me to do to that big beautiful ass.”He grinned.

“Will you shut the fuck up and get serious for a moment.”

“Look, you got my word.”

“You know what? You’re a Fuck boy.”

“A Fuck boy? I’m confused. You were just saying that you would move to Texas with me and now I’m a Fuck boy?”

Jada knew that she was being contradictory and her emotions were all over the place. She wanted this man, but she didn’t quite believe that he wanted her in the same capacity.

She said to Fresh, “Look, baby, I’m sorry. I’m just getting older and I don’t have time for the bullshit. That’s all.”

“And I don’t either.”

***

Ava’s loft had twelve foot ceilings and exposed brick. The cherry-colored hardwood floors sparkled and Shamari guessed that it must have ran her a few thousand dollars a month. He wondered how she afforded such a nice place but then he remembered that she had run off with the D-boy’s money.

“Water or Pepsi?”Ava asked.

"Pepsi."

She grabbed him a Pepsi from the fridge and they sat at the bar. He accepted the soda and they sat at the bar on two barstools side by side. She said, "You know, I thought Jada was cool, but now I don't know if I like her."

He looked confused as he took a swig of his soda and said, "Where is this coming from?"

"She wants you."

"She made it clear who she wants."

"You don't know. You're not a female."

"She made it clear that she is with Fresh. That's who she wants to be with and that's who she is with."

"I've never met Fresh, but as a woman, I can tell you that she is probably insecure in some part of that relationship."

"What happened?"

"She come asking me if I had fucked you."

"What did you tell her?"

"I denied it because it's none of her business."

Shamari grinned. He was happy that it was obvious that she was jealous of his and Ava's relationship. She had hurt him and she deserved to be hurt.

Ava stood and tiptoed over the hardwood floors to the other side of the room to turn on the thermostat. She said, "There is something that you need to know about me."

"What?"

"I might look like a sweet innocent girl, but I can fight, Shamari, and I'll fuck your girl up."

"She can fight too, but I'm not going to let it get that far. I'll have a talk with her."

"You need to."

"I thought you guys were friends?"

"I just met her. I thought she was cool. She said it was okay if I dated you. I would have never dated you unless she said it was cool. But now that we are dating, she has a problem with it."

"I'll talk to her."

***

Jada had tried to reach Shantelle for Fresh. He needed her to make the final run before he turned himself in. Jada had called her three times but her phone had gone to voicemail, so they decided to just stop by her home. Jada was about to knock on the door when she heard a man's voice say, "Bitch, I'll kill you."And then she heard Shantelle screaming and hollering.

She turned to Fresh and said, "We have got to do something."
"Do what?"
"Some dude is beating her ass. Can't you hear it?"
"I'm minding my own business. I already got problems."
The door flew open and there stood a coal-colored, buffed guy with biceps bulging from a tiny-ass Superman T-shirt. The man had hoop earrings in both ears and was wearing some kind of ugly-ass silver mood ring. He was a weird motherfucker for sure.
The big, black super hero said, "What the fuck do y'all want?"Shantelle stood behind the man crying.
"Shantelle, what's wrong?"
Shantelle said, "Please, Jada, just go."
The black super hero said, "You heard what she said."
Fresh stepped in between Jada and the super hero and said, "Look, you're going to learn how to talk to my lady. I don't give a fuck what you do in that house, but you are going to respect my woman."
The super hero laughed and said, "Or what? What the fuck are you going to do to me, nigga? I'll toss your skinny ass across the street."
Fresh pulled out a black Glock 19, cocked it, and aimed it at the super hero's motherfuckin' dome. The super hero panicked and kneeled while waving his hands in a surrender motion.
"Please, bruh, don't kill me. I got kids, man. Don't kill me. Please."
Fresh said, "Get your bitch ass up and get the fuck away from here."
"But I got clothes in her apartment."
"Buy you some new ones."
Shantelle said, "Don't come back."Then she invited Jada and Fresh inside. Shantelle was wearing some really skimpy green gym shorts

that were gripping her ass and revealing her well-defined legs.

"Let me go cover up some more."

"Yes, please do that," Jada said then she looked at Fresh to see if he was looking at Shantelle but he wasn't—he had already stolen a look.

Shantelle returned wearing some tight jeans and Jada wanted to tell the ho to go change again but she didn't.

"What was that all about?"

"He's such a lame."

"That's obvious," Fresh said.

"Yeah, I started working at Live Fitness as a personal trainer and I guess you could say we started fucking around. I let him spend a few nights. He would get jealous if he saw me laughing with male clients or co-workers. But anyways. What brings you over here?"

Fresh said, "I know you used to make runs for Trey, and I was wondering if you could make a quick run for me."

"I can do that. God knows I need the money."

"Well, it will be this weekend sometime."

"Let me know. I'm down."

Fresh thanked her and Jada hugged her and said, "If you have any more problems out of big dude, call us."

Fresh said, "No, call the police because I will kill that nigga. I don't need the trouble."

"I don't think I'll have any problems from him again. I'm going to take his clothes to work and then take out a restraining order."

Shamari was jerking off to an Instagram model's video when Hunch barged into Shamari's room unannounced and startled Shamari. "What the fuck?"

"Look, bruh, some dude out here on the porch, said his name was Big Ced. Says he knew your boy Black and he wants to talk to you." Shamari's forehead wrinkled. He didn't know anybody named Big Ced. He knew a couple of guys named Ced but none of them were big. He tucked his penis in his underwear, sprang from the bed, slipped into a pair of sweatpants and a tee. He then stepped out on the porch. A huge man stood on the porch and two more men were waiting in the car. Shamari introduced himself.

"Yo. I know I don't know you. Why are you showing up at my sister's house?"

Ced laughed and said, "Whoa, I'm a friend of Black's. I got shot hanging out with the nigga a few weeks before he was murdered. I've known him since we were kids."

"And tell me what the fuck does that have to do with me?"

"I think I know who did it."

"Detroit dudes?"

"No, I think it was some dudes from L.A. Bruh, Black had a beef with some dudes from L.A. He went to the county jail and he got into a fight with a few of them, and I'm telling you, bruh, I think they killed Black."

"What?"

"Yes."

"Okay, what do you want me to do about it? I'm out on bond waiting on a re-trial for a fed case."

"Black spoke highly of you and he said that you were one of the realist dudes he ever been around."

Shamari crossed his arms. "So wassup, Big Ced?"

"Black was feeding the hood and ever since he got murdered, I ain't been eating, you feel me?"

"You think I'm a plug?"Shamari laughed. "I'm a grown man living at my sister's house."

"I'm just looking for anything. It don't have to be what Black gave me. You can just throw a dog anything."

Shamari looked over Ced's shoulder at the two clowns in the cherry-colored Impala blowing trees playing Future's TRAP NIGGAS blasting through the speakers.

"So this how you get down, Ced? You show up at my sister's house with strange niggas and I don't know none of y'all and you ask me for work?"

"It's not like that at all. They think I'm here to get the screen on my iPhone fixed. I told them that you fix cracked screens and shit."

"Why did you bring them in the first place? Why ain't you driving?"

"I had to sell my car, bruh. I'm telling you, I ain't eating."

"Damn! You couldn't have been eating that much if Black been gone a few months and now you tapped out."

"I just dropped twenty stacks down on a house for my baby mama and I got other kids. Eight in all. You feel me? Black had some money that belonged to me. He never told me where he got the work from, but I assumed it was Cali or Texas somewhere. So I asked could I send my money with him. I'd given him twenty thousand and you know the rest."

 One of the clowns got out of the car. He was a tall, ebony-colored, skinny man with dirty-looking braids and black-assed lips. "Ced, ask the homie if he can fix a cracked iPad screen."

"See what I mean? They don't know shit."

Ced yelled, "No, the screen is too big."

The man ducked back into the car.

Ced said, "Look, Shamari, I know you don't know me, but me and Black were good friends bruh!"

"It's funny he never mentioned you."

"Do your research. I know his whole family. His pops Bankhead Bo, his sister Rashida, his grandma Nana, and his kids. All of his kids."

Clearly, the man knew Black, Shamari figured and shook his hand. Ced passed him an old iPhone and said, "My number is in here. If you run down on anything, hit me up. I'm starving out here and if you need me to do anything, man, I'm down. Black said you were like a brother. A brother of Black's is a brother of mine."

***

Gordo sent Shantelle back to Atlanta with one hundred kilos. She drove to Fresh's house as soon as she got back to Atlanta to meet Fresh and Jada. Fresh unloaded all the work and then invited Shantelle inside. He then paid her ten grand.

"Look, Fresh, I really appreciate this.""No problem. Hey, I wanted to ask you a question."
"Anything."
"It's about Q."
Shantelle huffed. "I don't like him."
"I know. I just want to ask you a question."
"Okay."
"Do you think that Q influenced the crazy white bitch to kill Trey?"
"That I don't know. But do I think it's possible? Yes. I don't think Q is a good person. He tried to kill me."
Jada interrupted, "And you want me to get this motherfucker out of jail?"
"What?"Shantelle said. "Look, Fresh, I really wanted to make some extra money but anything involving Q, I don't want to be a part of it."
"I understand," Fresh said then he turned to Jada and looked at her. His eyes said, "Why in the fuck did you want to bring that shit up for?"
"Shantelle, I appreciate what you did. I really do and it's your choice if you don't want to help. But understand, I didn't know Trey."
"I loved Trey."
"So did Starr."
"What is that supposed to mean?"
"Trey was no angel."
"I understand that, but your man wanted to kill me for telling the truth."

84

"I've been knowing Q all of my life, so while he wanted to murder Trey and it might be fucked up, he is my man."

"I get that. And I'm just letting you know that I don't want to have shit to do with him."

"I can respect that."

***

TeTe had whipped her Range Rover into a gas station and hopped out of the car. She sprinted inside to get some strawberry Trident gum before pumping gas. She had just placed the gas pump inside the gas tank when a man on the other side of the pump said, "TeTe, that's a nice Range Rover you have. Is the engine turbo?"

TeTe lowered her sunglasses and realized that she didn't recognize the stranger. The attractive black man stood in front of a blue Ford Focus.

She raised her eyebrow. "You know me?"

He flashed his FBI badge and said, "I'm Barry Daniels with the FBI. A good friend of Black's. I'm sure he told you about me. Or maybe not."

"What the hell do you want?"

He inched toward TeTe. The gas pump was still in the gas tank. He lit a cigarette and she stepped back. Who the fuck lights cigarettes near gas pumps?

When he saw her fear, he dropped the cigarette then stamped it out. "Did I scare you?"

"What the fuck do you want?"

"I wanna talk."

"About?"

"I need help."

"I'm not a trapper."

"I know."

"I have nothing to say to you."

"Here's what I want."He paused, "You seem like a very enterprising woman so I want you to introduce me to some people and we can take over the streets together. And I'll cut you in on the profits."

"Look, you're the Feds. I'm sure you bust guys every day. Why do you need me?"

"Look, I know you can help me."

"But I'm not."

"Then I'll just shut that little escort service of yours down."

"Look, man, you need to get away from me before I scream."

He passed her a card and said, "TeTe, call me." He lit another cigarette and winked at her then jumped into his car and drove away and pulled up Jada's contact information.

Shamari sat on the passenger side of Jada's Benz with his seat reclined. Jada lowered the volume of her radio and said, "TeTe had a visit from your boy the other day."

"Who?"
"Daniels."
"Who the fuck is that?"
"The FBI agent."
"Who is TeTe?"
"Black's ex. I keep telling you about her."
"Was she at the funeral?"
"She was."
"I want to meet her."
"She's crazy. I'm warning you."
Shamari lowered the visor where he found a mirror on the passenger side of the car. A long strand of hair spiraling from his nostril. He yanked it out and said, "You didn't tell me that your boy was on the run."
"He told you?"She sounded surprised that Fresh had told him.
"Yeah."
She turned and faced him. "I'm sorry."
"You should have told me."
"I know."
 His grabbed her hand and held it for a while. She turned to him, their eyes met and for a moment, there was sexual energy between them. She pulled her hand back.
"Jada, you're going to have to stop taking chances for people. One of these days your luck is going to run out."
"You're right."
"You have a good heart."
"I know."
"You can't save the world, baby."
"He's going to turn himself in."

"Bullshit. If he was going to turn himself in, he would have done it by now."

"You think so?"

"Jada, use your brain. Don't be dick dumb. Women get fucked good and forget all about common sense."

"I believe him."

"I don't."

"You don't like him, do you?"

"Actually, I think he's cool. I hate the fact that he has the woman I love, but there is nothing I can do about that, can I? You made your choice."

Jada knew it was time to change the subject. "The FBI dude that came to see TeTe threatened to shut her down unless she helped him."

"She runs a ho house?"

Jada laughed and said, "It's an escort service. High-end bitches."

"He knows about it?"

"Obviously."

"What does he want her to do?"

"Wants her to help him move drugs, but she would never lie in bed with him. She is convinced that he had something to do with Black's death, but there is no way for her to prove it."

Shamari said, "What's up with this guy? Why the fuck won't he go away?"

***

Jada had given Shamari TeTe's number. He called her and said that he would like to meet with her. She gave him directions and he drove right over. His first thought when he saw her was that there was no way that this woman was in her mid-forties. The second thought was there was no way she was as gangster as Black had told him she was.

His eyes were on her svelte figure. The black dress was painted on her and the Louboutin shoes made her look very tall. He would absolutely fuck her if the opportunity presented itself. Black was gone, so there would be no problems.

88

She invited him in and said, "Nobody warned me that you were so sexy," she said, admiring his buffed body.

He smiled and inhaled her Tom Ford perfume.

"Would you like something to eat?"She winked, then flashed a smile.

"I'm fine."

"At least have a drink with me."

"Okay, what do you have?"

"What do you want?"

"Henny."

 She led him to the bar and poured two glasses of Hennessy.

"Madam TeTe."

She smiled. "You have kind eyes."

He smiled and said, "I've never heard that before."

"I can read people. It's one of my gifts."

"Oh, really?"

"Yes. You think I'm bullshitting you, don't you?"

"I don't know."

"You tend to care about people more than they care about themselves."

"Sometimes."

He took a swig of the Henny.

"So what brings you here?"

"I came to talk about Black."

Her eyebrows rose. "What about him?"

He downed the Hennessy and she poured him another shot.

"There was this detective…well, FBI agent, that came by my sister's house and said he worked with Black. He wanted to work with me. Says he helped get me out."

"Black guy?"

"Yeah. Do you know him?"

"He approached me at the gas station."

"What do you think about him?"

"I don't."

"You don't what?"

"I don't think about him. I got more important shit to do than to worry about some cop. I told Black not to fuck with him, but he said that it was a means to an end. Said that dude would take work from dealers and give it to him."

"What did Black say about him? Was he a'ight?"

"Black didn't say much. I don't know if he was a'ight or not, but he did help us get my daughter back when she was kidnapped. Well, he gave us some counterfeit money to give to the kidnappers.

"Okay."

"You're not thinking of dealing with this dude, are you?" Shamari sipped his Hennessy. "I didn't want to get back in the game, but I just had to realize I am what I am."

"You sound like Black."

"I mean, what else is a motherfucker supposed to do?"

"There are other ways to make money."

"I don't know them. I know what I know. One more thing. Did Black ever mention a dude named Big Ced?"

"Yes, he mentioned him a time or two. I never met him."

"What did he say about him?"

"He was his homie. You know Black. He knew everybody in Atlanta."

"Yeah, part of his downfall."

"Really."

"Can you remember anything that he said about him?"

"Not much, but they were friends and toward the end of Black's life, he was working with Ced."

"Okay, so he's legit."

"I guess. Like I said, I never met him."

"He know Black's whole family."

"Like I said, Black never said anything bad about him. In fact, I think Ced got shot one night while hanging with Black."

"Ok. Good info."Shamari downed his drink, stood and offered his hand.

TeTe refused and said, "We're family, Shamari."She reached up to give him a hug.

He held on to her for a while and when he released her, she guided his hand down to her ass. Damn, she was scandalous, but he had to admit, the old bitch turned him on.

***

The motorcycle sounded like it was on the next street over.
The sun had just gone down and Big Ced and his two friends,
Dante and a guy named Hen, were playing craps. Big Ced was
shaking the dice, about to roll the dice when Shamari rode up
on the Black Kawasaki Z800. Ced stood when Shamari
approached.

"Damn that's a nice bike, bruh."
Shamari grinned. "I just got it a few weeks ago."
"Did you have a hard time finding us?"
"Not at all."
Ced introduced Shamari to Hen and Dante.
Shamari recognized Dante from when Ced had visited his sister's
house. He had never seen Hen. Dante was the man with the black
assed lips that had gotten out of the car at his sister's house.
"Can we talk for a moment?"
"Yeah, let's go in the house."
Ced passed Dante the dice and led Shamari inside the house.
Once they were on the inside of the house they sat at Ced's
granny's kitchen table said. "I did a background check on you."
Ced said. "And what did you find out?"
"I heard you were thorough."
"I told you that but, my question is how am I going to eat bruh?
Black is gone I need some money and some money fast."
"Let's get one thing straight."
Ced looked confused. "What?"
"Don't you ever come over my sister's house again, with a gang of
Niggas. You feel me?"
"That was my bad bruh. I'll never do that."
Shamari removed a backpack from his back dumped the contents
of it on the little rickety table—A ziplock bag wrapped in gray
tape. A half of a kilo of pure coke.
Ced eyeballed the package "What is this for? How much do you
want back?"
"It's a gift."
"For what?"

"Look I'm back in the business. I've been gone for a while and I'm going to need enforcers."
Ced said, "Look bruh I'm a hustler I ain't some kind of bodyguard, but since you were friends with Black, any kind of problem you have becomes a problem of mine."
"And that's all I ask. But I want you to help me find these L.A. dudes that killed Black. I promised his Dad that I would take care of that for him."
Ced gave Shamari a pound and said, "We will."

Plies's RAN OFF ON THE PLUG TWICE was playing at a table in the VIP section inside the strip club Magic City. Stunna had thrown about fifty thousand dollars in the air. Making it rain baby! Stunna, Micky, Micky's girlfriend Kelsey and four other dudes had three tables at Magic City with fifty thousand dollars on each table. Around one a.m., he told Micky that he was leaving.

"Okay. I'm going to stay here for a few more minutes."
"You want me to leave Blue here with you?"
"No, I'm good."
Forty-five minutes later, Stunna was gone and Goldie, Micky's stripper girlfriend, plopped on Micky's lap.
 A man named New York approached the section. New York had a square jaw and bushy eyebrows. He grabbed Goldie's hand, and said, "Let me talk to you for a second."
Micky smacked his hand.
The man smirked and said, "She with you? Who the fuck you 'posed to be?"
Goldie turned to the man. "Let me finish here and I'll be with you in a second."
"Yeah, man."Micky grabbed a handful of money from the table and tossed it at the man and said, "Go get your own girl."
The man laughed. "Bitch, don't think you a dude because you look like one. Don't get yourself fucked up."
 Goldie bounced from Micky's lap and approached the man and said, "You don't want these problems. Trust me her brother will hurt you."
"I don't give a fuck who her brother is."A short pie-faced man wearing dress shoes approached the man and took him by the arm and said. "Chill New York.". New York turned to the man and said "Get your motherfuckin' hands off me."
Then one of the bouncers had heard all of the commotion, grabbed New York and escorted him out of the club.

Goldie took her position on Micky's lap and kissed her.

"You coming home with us tonight?"Micky asked.

"Not tonight. I have to get my son ready for school in the morning."

"I feel ya. Thanks for trying to de-escalate that situation because it was about to get ugly for that nigga."Micky flashed her black .380 Ruger.

"No problem."

***

Shamari had just finished five sets of pushups, a kettlebell workout, and some calisthenics. The tiny wifebeater struggled to contain Shamari's pecs. And his triceps looked damned good to Ava. He smiled when she entered his sister's home. His sister and Hunch had gone to the movies to see BATMAN V SUPERMAN.

"You okay, babe?"

"No, I'm not okay."

"What's wrong?"

"There are people after me."

"What kind of people? Who are these people and why are they after you?"He knew that there were people after her but he wanted to see if she would be honest with him about what she had done.

"It's a long story."

"We have nothing but time, baby."

"When I lived in North Carolina, I was fucking around with this D-Boy named Mario and I took some money from him."

"You took the man's money?"

"I know. I was wrong for doing it."

"You damn right you were wrong for that. How much did you take?"

"A million dollars."

"You took a million dollars!"Shamari stood and paced. "What the fuck? Why did you take it?"

"I'm not a thief. I was listening to my friends and they convinced me to do it."

Shamari laughed and said, "That peer pressure excuse don't fly once you're over twenty-five."

She started crying. "I fucked up and I think about this every day of my life. I was wrong for what I did. I know I was."

"So what made you decide to tell me this?"

"I just wanted to be honest with you. I like you. I haven't met anyone like you in a long time."

He sat down beside her on the bed and he kissed her. He told her it was going to be okay and that everyone made mistakes. He took hold of her hand and pulled her onto the bed. He collapsed on the bed and she was now on top of him. The left hand gripping her ass and the right tugging at her dress.

"What are you doing?"

"What do you think?"

"In your sister's house?"

"Why not?"

"You gotta get outta here."

"And you gotta get out of that dress."

 Her smile revealed deep dimples. "Take me out of it then."

He unzipped the back then unhooked her bra and tossed it on the bed. His dick swelled after seeing her perfect little boobies, they were just a handful and he loved that.

She stood then removed the dress then took the bra off the bed and lay it on the chair across from the bed. She stood in front of him with a pink G-string.

He removed it with his teeth, and seconds later, he was staring at her kitty.

"I love lavender."

She smiled.

He seized her waist, bringing her close and kissed her kitty again. Then he licked the lips and asked, "How do you want me to make love to you?"

She laughed. His attentiveness fascinated her. "I want you to fuck me. But first lick my clit."

He licked her gently and he gnawed at it. She resisted and he knew she didn't like it. He picked her up and lay her on the bed and

nibbled on her clit until she clawed his back, ripping his wifebeater off his torso. His V-shaped taper aroused her. His abdomen was chiseled like a super hero in a comic book. She imagined him doing sit-ups and pullups and pumping iron on the prison yard.
"Take your pants off, bae. Fast."
He removed his pants and then his boxers and his dick swelled even more and it was long and it hooked slightly left. He drove his penis down her throat as she took hold of his ass. She was uninhibited and he liked that. She removed his dick from her mouth and licked his balls, then his asshole. His face reddened then he struggled to break free from her grip.
"Whoa," he said.
"What's wrong?"she said, smiling.
"You just caught me off guard."
"You don't like it?"
"I don't."
"I won't do it then."
"I'll do you, but I'm not that kind of man."
 She giggled at the thought that at least she didn't have to ever wonder what he did in prison. She laughed again and then went back to work until he couldn't take it any longer. He thrust her onto the bed and went deep inside her. She moaned and he plunged deeper.
She said, "Hard and rough. Don't take it easy on me."
He flipped her over and she arched her back, poking her ass out. He entered her from behind as he took hold of her beautiful, natural hair.
"You slut! You ho! Bitch, you!"
She was aroused. He knew how to fuck her the way she wanted to be fucked and she loved that. He removed his dick and she sucked him again and he was hard again in seconds.
"I want more," she said.
"Damn, girl."
"I'm telling you, I haven't been fucked in a while."
"I need some water."
She made a sad face.
"I promise you, after I down the water, we can go for round two."
She was smiling hard as hell.

***

Micky's hand grabbed Kelsey's thigh while waiting on a red light. They kissed and proclaimed their love for one another.

"This has been the best eight months of my life."
"Mine too," Micky said."
"When are we going to get married?"
"I don't know. I want to soon."
"What about Goldie?"
"What about her?"
"I want you for myself."Kelsey said. "And to be honest, I'm getting tired of this threesome shit."
Micky leaned over, kissed Kelsey and said, "Relax, babe, we're going to work it out. I promise."
The driver of a silver Volvo SUV honked the horn interrupting the flow of the conversation then the light turned green. Micky took off and then exited I-285 headed to Sandy Springs. She noticed a black Altima that she had seen on Peachtree.
"I think we're being followed," Micky said.
Seconds later, she was cut off by a white Dodge Ram. She crashed into the truck and the Altima blocked her in. Four men got out of the car. Micky reached for the gun under her seat but didn't feel it. A rail-thin man with receding braids smashed the window. Guns were drawn. Big guns. The kind of guns that would annihilate Micky and Kelsey. Kelsey and Micky were yanked out of the car and tossed into the truck. They were driven to an alley in a remote location and tossed out of the car into the street.
Micky recognized one of the men. The guy that had been talking shit to her in Magic City.
"Remember me, bitch?"
"Fuck you!"
"No, fuck you."The man unbuckled his pants.
"What are you doing?"Micky asked.
The man stood over Micky and said, "I'm 'bout to show you that you're a bitch and you need to stay in a bitch's place."
 He inched closer to her and she kicked his shin. She scrambled to get away but two men restrained her.

Kelsey lunged onto one of the men's back and clawed his face with her long nails before being slammed hard to the pavement on her pretty little face.

Micky cried out.

"No need of crying now, bitch. You want to be a man."

"No man do this," Micky said. "Do you know who my brother is? If you fuck with me, I swear to God, Stunna will kill all of y'all."

"Fuck you and Stunna. Right now, only God can save you," the man said then tucked his dick back in his drawers. "There is only one way out. Tell me where some work is and I won't fuck your manly ass. If you don't tell me where the work is, you are surely getting fucked today."

"I ain't telling you where shit is."

Kelsey said, "I will take you to the house. Please don't hurt her."

New York moved toward her and said, "Where is her house? Where does she live?"

Micky looked at Kelsey. Her facial expression said, Bitch, why did you open your mouth?

The two men were still restraining Micky. New York removed his dick from his pants. "Rip that bitch's clothes off."

"You said you weren't going to hurt her."

"I lied. This bitch is going to get fucked tonight."

"No. No. No. Don't do it."

Micky's eyes teared up.

DeSean Cummings lay on his stomach while Ava gave him a back massage. He was crying and when Ava noticed him crying, she asked him what was wrong, but he didn't answer. She sprang from the bed and said, "Did something bad happen?"

He stood and grabbed his shirt from the chair. "No."
She kept pressing. He had requested her six times and she considered him not just a client, but a friend. He grabbed a robe from the door and stepped into the bathroom. She overheard him bawling and it was freaking her out. Rarely did she see a grown-ass man crying. She burst into the door and he stared at his reflection in the mirror.
She draped her arms around him. She wanted to console him to let him know that everything was going to be all right. His tears trickled down his face.
"Nobody wants me."
"What are you talking about?"
"I was waived from the team."
"Waived? What the hell does that mean?"
"I was cut."
"That's not the end of the world."
"Nobody else has picked me up and my agent says it might be over for me. Nobody wants to deal with me. It's the end of my world. This is all I have done since I was a little boy. What else can I do?"
"You have money."
"I have money but not a purpose."
"What about your children?"
"You don't understand."
"You're right. I don't understand how a grown man, a spoiled-ass rich millionaire, could be crying because he got cut from a team. There are people out here with some real-ass issues, my friend."
"And I'm not saying they don't, but this is my issue."

"You need to get it together!"she yelled and it surprised him. She knew that this was not what he wanted to hear, but it was what he needed to hear.

"I'm twenty-eight and washed up."

"So when did you plan to retire?"

"I never wanted to retire."

She said, "Look, you live a good life. You have a wife and kids. Whether you play football or not, life is good."

"You don't understand."

"You're right."

"I've been playing since I was eight years old. This is my life."

She now felt bad for him. His self-worth was tied up in a silly-ass game.

He exited the bathroom and she trailed him. He grabbed a bottle of Hennessy that sat on the nightstand and poured a glass. "Do you think you can call your friend?"

"You have coke."

Picking up his pants that were lying on the floor, he found an eight ball. "I forgot about this."Then he drank more liquor and then he said, "I need more."

"More what?"

"More white girl."He dug into his pockets and handed her a thousand dollars. "Go get me an ounce."

"That's too much."

His eyes pleaded with her soul. He was in hell. He absolutely needed her at this moment. She was against self-medication, but the way his eyes looked, he needed this coke to save his life.

"Please do it."

She slid into her jeans, which had been lying on a chair across the room. Three minutes later, she bolted out of the door and called Jada.

"I need some white girl."

"Where are you?"

"I'm at the Four Seasons again."

"I'll meet you at the bar in an hour."

"Okay, perfect. "

Forty-five minutes later, Jada called and asked Ava what she would be wearing. She wanted to spot her easily in a crowd.

"A pair of jeans and wifebeater."

"Perfect. See you in fifteen."

Fifteen minutes later, Ava strolled into the bar searching for Jada who had told her that she was sitting at the bar having a martini. She scanned the room and the first person she saw was Shamari. He approached her.

She asked, "What are you doing here?"

"I'm supposed to meet some girl for Jada." Then he looked her over once and said, "Oh damn, it was you that wanted the coke. What the fuck?"

"I can explain."

"So you're here to sell ass?"

Ava was fuming and her eyes were pleading and hoping Shamari would understand. That goddamned Jada had set her up. How would she explain to Shamari that she had been working as a high-class escort? She really liked him. Damn!

***

It was 3.56 a.m. when Starr's phone rang.

"Hello?"

"Hello, baby."

She sat up in the bed and looked at the clock. "Who the fuck is this?"

"It's me, Q."

"I don't want to talk to you. How did you call me?"

"I just got out."

"What?"

"Yes, I just bonded out and I want to see you."

"I don't want to see you."

"I have shit I want to explain to you."

"There is no need." She ended the call and wondered how in the fuck did he get out.

***

Stunna staggered out of the bed and picked his phone up from the dresser. He saw that he had sixteen missed calls. His phone had been on silence. Blue had called him eight times. He dialed him.

"What's up?"
"I'm at the hospital."
"What's wrong? Is it Noni?"
"No. Micky got raped last night."
"What? Hell no. Who did it?"
Stunna started pacing and his heart was beating fast. Who had raped his sister? Who was dumb enough to fuck with her? Had she been somewhere running her mouth? What kind of nigga rapes a dyke? None of this shit mattered to him at this moment. Somebody had raped his sister and they had to be dealt with. Somebody had to pay with their life. He put on his shoes and was running out the house before he realized that he didn't have any pants on. He calmed himself down. He decided to take a shower and then headed to the hospital.

It was eight a.m. in the morning and Jada was backing out of her garage to head to the gym when she noticed a man in the rearview mirror standing behind her. He approached the side of the car and she lowered the window. "Can I help you?"

"Yes, Jada, I just need a moment of your time."
"Who are you and how the fuck do you know my name?"
He flashed his badge. "I'm FBI Agent
Barry Daniels."
She sighed and said, "And what the fuck do you want with me?"
"Can we go inside for a moment?"
 She looked around. There was nobody outside, but it would be just a matter of time before one of her nosey-ass neighbors came outside. She parked the car and they walked inside.
"I would offer you some water, but I don't want you to stay."
He laughed and examined her body. "You're more gorgeous than I thought you would be."
"What can I help you with?"
"I want you to get Shamari or Fresh to work with me."
"Please, you'd have a better chance of curing cancer than having me approach anybody for you."
"It's in your best interest."
"It's in your best interest to get the hell out my house."
"Look, I helped Shamari get out of prison."
"That's Shamari's problem, not mine."
"Jada, I'm going to offer you a deal. Help me and I'll help you. I promise not to send the cops to get Fresh. After all, he is a wanted man. A double murder in the state of Texas is not a good look."
"Do what you gotta do."
"Now, you're going to force me to use my hole card."
"And what card is that?"
He removed a cellphone from his pocket. "You know what this is?"
"A phone."
"Not just anybody's phone."

"Whose phone is it?"

"Black's."

"Okay, you got Black's phone."

"What do you think Fresh is going to say if I show him this phone?"

"I don't know and I don't give a fuck."

Daniels powered on the phone and scrolled to the text messages and said, "Here is a text message from you."

Jada looked at the phone and read the message she had sent Black. BLACK, YOU WERE AMAZING LAST NIGHT. I HAVEN'T BEEN FUCKED LIKE THAT IN A LONG TIME. NOW EVERY TIME I THINK OF BRYSON TILLER'S SONG 'DON'T', I'M GOING TO THINK ABOUT YOU. COME OVER TONIGHT AND FINISH WHAT YOU STARTED.

Daniels looked at her. "Damn! I don't know if Fresh or Shamari is going to take this too well."

Jada's mouth flew open and she sat down and said, "How did you get this? You killed Black, didn't you?"

KINGPIN WIFEYS III,

PART 2: THE AGREEMENT

Shamari stared at Ava with an intensity that could cut through glass. Her eyes were pleading. She liked him and she didn't want him to walk out of her life. Jada had set her up, but she should have known that the hating-ass bitch would have told him about her job. She was his ex and she still wanted him. She stepped toward Shamari and attempted to grab his hand.

He folded his arms and said, "So do you have the money for the product?"

She handed him the money and asked, "Can I talk to you?"

"Shawty, there is nothing to talk about. You do what you do to take care of yourself. You're not my lady."

"I know I'm not your lady, but I can explain."

"Explain what?"

He passed her the coke and she dropped it into her purse.

"There is nothing to explain," he said.

"So you don't want to talk to me?" She wanted to cry. She didn't want to lose him, but he was right, they were not a couple. But her being in a hotel with a man looked cheap.

She tried to grab his shoulder and he pushed her back and said, "Don't touch me."

Shamari walked through the bar of the hotel into the lobby. She tailed him, calling out his name but he didn't answer. She watched him walk through the hotel door. She carried the coke back up to the room and DeSean was passed out.

She lay on the bed next to him and she texted Shamari sixteen times before he responded.

Shamari: WOULD YOU PLEASE QUIT TEXTING ME.

Ava: WOULD YOU JUST AGREE TO TALK TO ME.

Shamari: ABOUT WHAT?

Ava: I KNOW YOU'RE MAD AT ME.

Shamari: REALLY.

Ava: YES.

Shamari: SHOULDN'T I BE?

Ava: I DON'T KNOW. CAN WE JUST TALK?
Shamari: DON'T TEXT ME.
Ava: I'M GOING TO TEXT YOU UNTIL I GET A CONVERSATION OUT OF
YOU.
Shamari: DO WHAT YOU WANT TO DO, SHAWTY.

*****

The white Maserati whizzed through traffic and, exceeding speeds
120 miles per hour. Stunna lowered the top on the convertible
and the wind smacked his face. He knew there were cops out, but
right now he couldn't give a fuck about a trooper. His baby sister
had been violated. How did it happen? Who did this to his baby
sister? He dialed Kelsey's phone six times and each time he got her
voicemail: THIS IS MICKY AND KELSEY'S PHONE. WE'RE NOT
AVAILABLE RIGHT NOW, PLEASE LEAVE A MESSAGE AND WE WILL
GET RIGHT BACK TO YOU—Dyke shit. He cursed.
When he'd first realized that his sister was a lesbian, he was
surprised he'd never seen it coming. He wondered why did his
sister have to be a dyke. He remembered talking to her when she
was eleven when he had found her lusting after girls on the
Internet. He had asked her what she was doing and she said she
was admiring the girls, but he could see in her eyes that it was
much more than admiration.
A year later, she had barged into his room. She needed to talk to
him. He was sixteen at the time and he had been bagging the ten-
dollar sacks of marijuana that he would take to school and peddle
to rich kids.
She stood there wearing pink Hello Kitty onesie pajamas, rocking
side to side nervously.
"What the hell do you have to talk to me about?" He barked at her
like any brother with an annoying little sister.
"I'm gay," she said.
"What do you mean, you're gay?"
"I like girls."
His mouth flew open as he stood from the desk, abandoning the
bags of weed. "What do you mean that you are gay?"

"I'm gay." She smiled bashfully and then said, "I don't know how to say it more plain than I just said it. I'm gay and I wanted you to be the first person I tell."

"Like gay, gay?"

"I've always liked girls. I've tried to force myself to like boys, but I don't. When the other girls are talking about boys, I would try to talk about them too, but it seemed too awkward for me. I see guys that are fine as hell, but I think pretty much anybody can agree when someone is attractive. But attractive boys don't do it for me like attractive girls."

"You're thirteen."

"I'm twelve."

"You don't know what you want. You're too young to know that."

"I know and I know I don't like doing girly things."

He sighed and said, "I thought you had a crush on Jay?"

She laughed and said, "He does like me. Look at me, I'm cute. But I don't like him. Or any guy. I like Melody."

"Is Melody gay?"

"No, she likes guys."

"And why did you tell me this?"

She gave him strong eye contact. "I love you and I don't want to disappoint you."

He embraced her and held her. When he let her go, he said, "You need to get rid of that punk-ass Hello Kitty onesie. If you're going to like girls, you can't be wearing that."

And from that day forward, Micky dressed like a boy and acted like one too.

Stunna whipped his car into the hospital parking lot and raced to the reception area.

Stunna barged into the hospital and was told by the nurse where his sister was being held. He took the elevator to the seventeenth floor and saw Goldie and Kelsey standing outside room 1719. Kelsey approached him and he asked, "Where is my sister and what the fuck happened?"

Kelsey was about to explain when Stunna spotted Goldie and he said, "Somehow, I know you had something to do with this."
She looked confused. "What? I would never do anything to hurt Micky. I was at the club when this happened."
"You think I trust you? You only want my sister because you're looking for a free ride."
"I got my own money."
"Shaking your ass at a club night after night. You're lazy and I told Micky to stay away from you a long time ago."
"Look, I know you're upset, but you can't be taking your frustration out on me!"
Stunna narrowed his eyes and said, "If I find out that you had something to do with this, you are a dead bitch. I'm telling you."
Kelsey pointed to Micky's room.
Stunna burst into the room to find two detectives standing on both sides of her bed.
Stunna said to the cops, "She don't want to talk to you right now." He rushed past the cops, a black cop and a Hawaiian cop, to hug his sister, who was lying in the bed wearing a light blue hospital gown. She had a cut above her right eye. He kissed her forehead before he sat on the edge of her bed.
She looked up at him and said, "I'm okay, brother."
The black cop's name was Collins. He was a horse-faced man with a drooping mouth and gross razor bumps. "Are you related to the victim?"
"He's my brother." Micky said.
 Collins turned to Stunna. "We're going to ask you to leave. We'll ask her a few questions then you are free to return."
"She told you I'm her brother. I ain't leaving!" Stunna stood from the bed and said, "No disrespect, officers, but she was raped and she don't feel like answering no questions bruh!"
Keahi, the Hawaiian detective said, "Somebody raped your sister, and our job is to get to the bottom of it and find out who did it."
Stunna exchanged stares with the two cops. "Look, she don't want to be bothered with this bullshit."
The black cop ignored Stunna and kneeled beside the bed, legal pad in hand. "What kind of car were they driving?"

Micky ignored the detective and buzzed the nurse. Moments later, they came charging in. Micky informed the nurse that she wanted the cops to leave.

When the police left, Stunna closed the door and kneeled beside Micky's bed and asked, "How long they been here?"

"Not long. Earlier there was someone here from the police with a rape kit."

"Huh?"

"You know getting DNA and stuff like that."

"How do you feel?"

"Violated! This man made me feel like I was a kid and he could do what he wanted to do to me. I thought I was strong, bruh. I thought I was strong."

He closed his eyes and took a deep breath. Tears welled in her eyes. She saw the pain in her big brother's face. She could tell that he was hurting for her. He was sad that this had happened. She couldn't hold back her tears. She'd begun to cry and Stunna wanted to cry, but he wouldn't allow himself to break down.

He hugged her and held her. "You know I'm going to get them. Don't worry." He patted her on the back, kissed her forehead and said, "I love you, sis."

"I know you do and I love you too."

*****

The doorbell rang. Fresh rolled over to pick up the iPhone that was plugged into the lamp on the ni   ghtstand. The phone said 5:45 a.m. He sat up in the bed and his mind began to race. Who in the fuck was at his door at this time of morning? The police! He hopped off the bed and entered the walk-in closet and searched for a pair of running shoes. He grabbed a pair of blue and white Asics. The doorbell rang again. If it were in fact the police, he was going to make them earn their pay today. They were going to have to catch him. Maybe it was Jada he thought but changed his mind. Jada would have called. She never showed up at his place unannounced.

He remembered the outside cameras and that there was a security monitor in the guest bedroom. With running shoes in his hands, he tiptoed over the cold hardwood flooring and opened the bedroom door, trying not to make a fuss. He eyeballed the monitor above the desk. The monitor revealed a black man in a gray T-shirt. The man's face was turned away from the camera. After deciding that it wasn't the police, Fresh sprinted to the door and said, "Who the fuck is it?"

"Me."

"Me? Who the fuck is me?"

"Q. Let me in."

Fresh peered through the peephole and recognized that it was Q. He opened the door.

Q said, "Yo, let me in, man. It's cold out here."

Fresh laughed and said, "Nobody told you to wear that baby-ass T-shirt."

"It's April. It's 'posed to be warm."

"We ain't in Houston, bruh."

They sat at the kitchen table. "How in the hell did you get out?"

"Chanel signed me out."

"Who?"

"The girl you set me up with. The bourgeoisie chick from Tennessee."

Fresh laughed. "You know my damn memory ain't the best. But I didn't know you were still kicking it with shawty. Damn, that's surprising. She don't seem like the kind of woman that would be down for a dude when he gets locked up."

"I begged. Promised that I would give her money. She signed me out, and I'll be on curfew until the trial comes up."

"Worried?"

"Should I be?" Q asked.

 Silence.

"You think I murdered Trey?" Q asked.

"I didn't say that."

"What are you saying, champ?"

"I don't know."

"If there is anybody that I'll tell the truth to, it will be you."

Fresh shrugged his shoulders and said, "Look, man, I don't know."

Q sighed. He was irritated and he said, "So what's up? What
happened to Black?"
"Don't nobody know. Word is he had a beef with some L.A. dudes
and some Detroit dudes."
"Doesn't surprise me. So what's up with your situation?"
"Self-defense. It was one of those situations where it was either
them or me. I had to do what I had to do."
"Word on the streets is that it was a deal that went sour."
"Something like that."
"What do you mean, something like that?"
"You remember Jabo?"
"Your homie?"
Fresh walked to the cabinet and removed a box of Raisin Bran
then sat down. He didn't want to talk about what happened that
day. He wanted to block it out; a good friend was dead and he
hadn't had a chance to give him his proper respects before he was
buried.
"You don't want to talk?" Q said.
"I don't." Fresh dug into his bowl of Raisin Bran and avoided Q's
eyes.
"Why were you there? Why were you trying to cop work
somewhere else?"
"You know the answer to that."
"What do you mean?"
"You told Diego not to sell me shit."
Q tapped the table. "I never told him that."
"Why did he cut me off?"
Q avoided Fresh's eyes and said, "Look, I was dealing with him and
I was going to kill him for what he did to Rico, but somebody beat
me to it."
"We're keeping secrets?"
"I was going to tell you at the right time."
Fresh kept eating his cereal as he eyeballed Q.
"I was wrong."
"You damn right you were. I needed product and I did some shit
that I wouldn't have done. Now one of my friends is gone because
you told Diego not to give me product."

Q stood and said, "Wait a minute. You can't blame me for some shit that you chose to do. Why didn't you come to me? I had product."

Fresh pushed his bowl aside. "Look, you were talking this shit about how I had to kill Black to prove to the wetbacks that I didn't kill Diego." Fresh laughed. "What's ironic is that you are telling me that you were planning on killing Diego your goddamned self. I don't feel like getting into this shit with you because you're pissing me the fuck off."

"I had plans to handle that situation."

Fresh said, "Look, man, if we are going to keep working together I'm going to need you to quit treating me like a kid."

"I was wrong." Q said. His eyes were sincere.

"Damn right you were wrong and for that I have a double murder charge to fight."

"I'll pay for your attorneys."

"It's not about you paying for my attorneys. Three lives were lost. This shit didn't have to happen."

"I'm sorry, but you know how shit goes in the street. If you didn't kill them, somebody else would have."

"I would rather it been somebody else," Fresh said. "One more question. Did you kill Trey?"

"No, I told you I didn't."

"Yeah, but you know what? I don't know if I believe you. It makes no sense. You say you wanted to kill him because you wanted to control the Atlanta drug game. You could have done that with him being your ally. Did you kill him because you wanted to control Atlanta or because you wanted Starr?"

"I didn't kill him."

"You sure? Because from what I've heard about Trey, he would never talk to the police.

"I know he didn't and I hate I wanted him dead, but I didn't kill him."

"Answer the question."

"I wanted him dead because I wanted to make a move on Starr, but I didn't kill him. Did I want him dead? Yes. Did I do it? No."

Barry Daniels walked into Jada's home and sat down on her loveseat without her permission. Jada thought Daniels was an attractive man, but she knew that he was a cop—one that couldn't be trusted. She paced and he watched her, enjoying the view of the alluring woman. The black yoga pants revealed her shelf-booty.

She said, "Are you going to say something or are you going to just stare at me and lust?"

He smiled and said, "I could watch you all day."

"I don't have all day. I have to go to the gym."

"Look, Jada, nobody has to know about this text message you sent to Black."

"Wait a minute. Can you tell me who the fuck you are and how do you know so much?"

"I've told you who I am and showed you."

"Ok, you're the FBI agent that came to TeTe's house and the one that has been bothering Shamari."

He smiled.

Jada walked back and forth. Daniels undressed her with his eyes, dying to see what was underneath those yoga pants.

Jada said, "Well, Mr. Barry Daniels. I have news for you. I'm not a drug dealer."

"You don't have to be a drug dealer but you and Black have a lot in common. Wanna take a guess what that is?"

"We are both from Atlanta and we both know a lot of people."

"Yes, you do."

Jada glanced at her watch. She did want to go the gym and she knew that the longer she talked to him, the more unlikely it was that she would go.

"Look, I need your help, Jada."

"I can't help you."

A creepy smile emerged on his face and she could imagine what this cornball was thinking. Jada sat down on an armchair and crossed her legs.

"What do you want?"

"When is Fresh bringing another shipment?"

"How do you know about Fresh?"

"I know everything."

"Did Black tell you about him?"

"You know Black wasn't that kind of person."

Jada narrowed her eyes. She knew that Black would never let Daniels know shit to hurt anybody.

"I don't know what Fresh is into."

"Imagine how you are going to look when he finds out that you were fucking Black right under his nose." He paused, then said, "Better yet, imagine when the indictments arrive." He smirked. "You're knee deep in the dope game, Jada. Some lucky dyke is going to lick that pretty little puss."

"I wasn't fucking Black."

"Let me read the text." He held the phone in front of his face. "I still feel you inside of me. I can't explain the range of emotions. I feel guilty for fucking you, yet I want you at the same time. I don't know if this was a mistake. Maybe I'm just horny, either way, come by tonight."

She cut him off. She didn't like hearing what she'd written and she hated the fact that Daniels had Black's phone. She was embarrassed about what she had said, but she'd meant every word. He'd been so amazing that night.

"Help me and I'll get rid of the phone."

"How do I know that?"

"You'll have to trust me."

"I don't trust the police."

"Jada, I'm just like you. I want the dope. Nobody goes to jail; nobody gets hurt. I'm here for the product."

"You'll destroy the phone?"

"I'll give you the phone."

"Let me think about it."

He stole a glance at her body, then handed her one of his cards.

"Let me let you get to the gym. The gym does your body so good."
He looked her over one more time, winked, and said, "Keep in
touch."

*****

Shamari had agreed to see Ava after she had texted him a
picture of her ass in a pink thong, claiming that she needed
him inside her. He drove to her place in twenty minutes. She
met him at the door, naked. They kissed and he removed his
mesh Nikes then his shorts, T-shirt, and boxers. He folded his
clothes and placed them on a table before chasing Ava over to
the front of the huge window where she was waiting with her
ass spread and her hands on the windowsill as Shamari took
possession of her waist and drove his tool deep inside her. A
group of construction workers working on the high-rise next
door looked and pointed at the two lovers. Ava wanted to give
them a show. They deserved a break from their mundane lives.
She wanted them to see Shamari punish her, humiliate her; she
wanted them to hear her call him daddy. She wanted his load
on her pretty face.

"Do what you want to do to me, daddy!"
Shamari kept pounding until his dick slipped out. She faced him.
He hoisted her against the cold, hard windowsill and plunged until
she felt his tool touching her navel. He kissed her every time he
stroked and she clawed his back with one hand and removed the
sweat from her face with her free hand.
He asked, "What do you want me to do?"
"Keep doing what you are doing."
"Let's go to the bed."
"I want them to hear me scream. I want them to see you punish
me."
Her kitty was dripping and it had become difficult to stay engaged.
They collapsed on the floor, out of the view of the men in the
building. He erupted on her belly. She used her fingers to massage
it in and then licked her fingers.

11

She stood. He was still lying on the floor with one sock on. He held onto his lifeless penis, stroking it while admiring her body.

She grinned when she saw him staring then she sprinted upstairs as he searched for his other sock that he'd lost during intercourse. She returned with two wet, warm towels. After she tossed him a towel, she cleaned herself up. She noticed the men in the building across the street giving her a thumbs up. She smiled and gave them a thumbs up then closed the blinds with the remote.

Shamari stood up and for the first time, she noticed that he had a nice ass. She wanted to smack it but thought that she was better off not doing that after she had tried to lick his ass a few weeks ago. He had warned her that he was not that kind of guy.

His boxers were folded and sitting on an end table. He slipped them on as she lusted after his chiseled body. He sat on the sofa and she sat on the opposite end. She looked into his eyes.

Shamari said, "You like putting on a show for the fellas in the next building?"

"This is the first time I've done this here."

"But you have done this before?"

She smiled. "Yes, why not?"

"Don't you worry they are going to look at you funny if you see them on the street?"

"I don't think about it, honestly. You know, Shamari, we all fuck. Every last one of us. Everyone fucks or thinks about fucking. Why should I be embarrassed about something that happens? We're young. Now is the time to have fun. I'm not going to have this body forever and neither are you."

"Do you ever see yourself getting married?"

Ava sighed. "I never thought about getting married, but I would like to, I suppose."

"You suppose?"

"I mean either way will be fine with me. If I get married, that would be cool, of course. But if I don't, I won't worry about it that's for damn sure. Why do you ask?"

"I don't know. I don't see a girl like you wanting to get married."

Ava frowned. "A girl like me? What the fuck is that supposed to mean?"

"I didn't mean nothing by it."

She frowned and said, "Look, can we talk about the other night?"
He huffed and said, I don't want to talk about it."
"Why not? I mean it's the only way we are going to get past what
happened."
"It doesn't mean anything."
"It does because I can tell you felt some kind of way about it."
"I didn't."
"You did."
He looked upward and said, "Okay, you want to talk? Talk."
"Look, I used to be a girl like Jada. You know I used to use men for
money and shit and I've sold pussy before. It's something that I'm
not proud of, but I have."
"I knew that the other night."
"Look, Shamari, I'm in a jam. I need to make some money and this
is what I chose to do. I chose to do this for a while. I'm not going
to make this a lifestyle."
"Looks like you have."
"If it makes you feel any better, I haven't slept with anybody
except you since we've been dating."
"It don't make me feel better."
"Look, I said what I had to say. And I like being with you and I want
to be with you. That's why when you say shit like a girl like me not
getting married. It hurts."
"I didn't mean it like that."
"Yes you did or else you wouldn't have said it." Ava stood and said,
"I'm the same kind of girl that Jada is and you wanted to wife that
ho." Her mood plummeted.
"Look, I'm sorry," he said.
"When you think about me, you think ho, right? And how Jada did
your ass. I'm not her."
"I never said that."
"I've done some shit that I ain't proud of; just like you have." She
paused and said, "You're a D-boy, Shamari."
"Ava, I'm sorry. It's that you seem like such a cool girl and I guess I
was thinking out loud cuz' I like you a lot and I want to find me
somebody and get serious with them but I can't get serious with
you."
"Why can't you get serious with me?"

“We just started seeing each other.”

“Excuses.”

 He sat on the sofa before locating his sock under the coffee table. He grabbed it and put it on. “I’m not making excuses.”

“Sounds like excuses to me.”

“You expect me to be your man after knowing you for one month?”

“No. I know how guys in Atlanta are. Especially black men. They have all these options, so the last thing on their mind is settling down.”

“Not true. Not for me anyway. I’m too old to play games.” Shamari said.

“And now you know how I feel.”

Shamari laughed. He couldn’t believe what he was hearing. This woman was selling her body for a living, and she wanted to settle down?

She smacked him in the face with a pillow. “What the hell are you laughing at?”

“I was just laughing.”

“You don’t think I’m wife material!”

“Whoa! You said yourself you didn’t care if you got married.”

“I never said that I wasn’t wife material. I said I don’t think about it. Forget being wife material. You don’t think I’m relationship material, do you?”

“I do.”

 Let’s be exclusive.”

“Quit doing what you are doing.”

“What am I doing?”

“Hoeing.”

“I’ll do that if we become exclusive. Are you ready to be with only me? If you are, I won’t see anybody else.”

He stared at her. He liked her but he wasn’t ready to commit to her. Hell, he just got out of prison. Why would he make a commitment like that right now?

She said, “I’m waiting on your answer.”

Silence.

*****

When Q walked into Starr's studio, she hopped from behind the counter and met him near the front of the studio. "What the hell are you doing here, Quentin?"

"Give me five minutes of your time. I won't take one second more."

"Leave right now." Her annoyance flared.

Brooke was flipping through her friends snaps on Snapchat when she heard the ruckus. She set her phone down.

"I want you to leave." Starr said.

"I ain't kill Trey."

"That's not for me to decide. You need to go."

Brooke was walking toward the front of the store to see if Starr needed help when Q spotted her.

He waved at her and said, "Everything is going to be okay, Brooke. I'm about to leave."

Starr turned to Brooke and said, "He is on his way out."

Brooke stepped behind the counter and started Snapchatting again.

"I didn't kill Trey. I didn't have him killed."

"All that shit about you wanting him dead because you wanted to be with me was straight-up bullshit, wasn't it?"

"No it wasn't."

"I'm not so special that anybody would kill to get me."

"Well, I wanted you and I wanted to take over Atlanta."

"You just needed a reason to kill him to justify it. Maybe you were a little jealous of him. I don't know."

"I never killed him."

"But you were going to."

"I told you that already."

"You should go."

"If this is about Trey, I've told you that I had wished he was dead. I wanted him dead but I didn't kill him."

"Q, it's not about Trey."

"Well then, what is it about?"

"Ever since you came around, there has been nothing but turmoil. You want to think of yourself as a good person, but you're not."

"I'm leaving."

"Then leave."

"Can I ask you one question?"

"What do you want?"

"You believe me, don't you?"

"Q, get the hell out of here. And how did you get out anyway? Last time I checked, you were having a problem getting someone to sign for you."

"What difference does it make to you?"

"None at all." She removed her phone, punched 911 into her phone without pressing send and showed it to him. "If you don't leave right now, I'm going to call the police."

He walked toward the front door and just before he left, he turned to her and said, "Hey! You have got to believe me. You have to."

"Go, Quentin, or I swear to God, I will call the police."

Later that evening, while T.J. was still at her parent's house, Starr invited Stunna over. He marveled over her home as he paced.

"I love this place."
He pressed his face against the glass as he looked out over the city. He could see his breath. He turned and faced her, and for the first time that evening, he noticed how gorgeous she was. She was dressed in distressed jeans, a pink blouse and pink Adidas. She looked kind of tomboyish, but so damn sexy at the same time.
"You look motherfuckin' amazing."
She laughed. "Nobody has ever said I look motherfuckin' amazing."
"Well, I'm telling you." He licked his lips and she felt chills travel her spine.
"How is Micky doing?"
"She's doing okay. I saw her last night. She's okay."
"You got any idea who did this to her? I mean who would want to—"
He cut her off. "Who would want to fuck a dyke, right?"
"That's what I thought, but there are a few sick motherfuckers out there that will do it."
"Has she ever been penetrated?"
"How the fuck am I 'posed to know that? I don't know. I haven't even thought about it. All I see is red right now. I'm going to find out who did this to my sister. Trust me."
"I'm just asking, babe."
His eyes lit up. "Babe?"
"Didn't mean it like that."
"I like it."
"Q came by the studio today," Starr said, changing the subject.
"Who?"
"My ex."
A scowl appeared on his face. "What was he there for?"

"To talk."

Stunna's face was confused. "Wanting to explain what? I thought you were done with him."

"I am."

"So why is he popping up at your place?"

Starr sensed a little jealousy in Stunna's voice. "Whoa, cowboy, why are you asking me all these questions about him?"

"I didn't mean it like that. You're right, I'll take it down a notch."

"Please."

Stunna said, "So you're going to tell me what happened between you and your ex?"

"Long story."

"We ain't got nothing but time."

Starr sighed, she didn't really want to get into the particulars of what happened, but she felt like she could trust him.

"Basically, Q used to supply my ex and after Trey was murdered, he made a move on me. I was vulnerable and I..." She paused. She felt like a slut for telling him that she had started sleeping with her boyfriend's friend. Would he judge her?

Stunna crossed his arms as he waited on her to finish her story. She bit down on her lips and said, "You'll judge me."

"I won't." He took possession of her hand and massaged it. "I don't have any room to judge anyone."

"I started sleeping with Q. Well, he became my man and then I found out that there was a possibility that he had Trey killed."

"What? Why?"

She felt guilty getting all into their business, but somehow Stunna made her feel comfortable. She felt like she could tell him anything.

"He said some bullshit like he wanted to kill him because he felt Trey was gonna talk to the police."

"Was he talking to PoPo?"

"Trey would never do that."

"The hardest motherfuckers fold."

"Trey cared too much about people. But, anyway, Trey's crazy, white baby mama killed him and now the police are investigating Q for coercing her to murder Trey."

"What? I've never heard of such a charge."

"I know."
Stunna paced and then said, "My head hurts now. I'm confused as
hell."
"Me too."
"Are you going to go back to him?"
"No."
"That's what I wanna hear." He smiled.

*****

Inside the penthouse suite, Ava wore patent leather heels and
a garter belt. She was dancing for David Peterson. Future's
song F UP SOME COMMAS played in the background. Dave sat
on the edge of the king-sized bed with his candy-striped
underwear down by his ankles. He stroked his penis as he
watched Ava's ass bounce from side to side.

"Can you twerk for me?"
She was bent over as she glanced back and smiled at him with
those gorgeous pearl white teeth. She said, "You want me to
twerk for you, daddy?"
He stroked his penis. "Yes."
"Say, please!" She flashed a smile.
Pre-cum formed at the tip of his penis. He kept stroking. "Please
twerk for me."
She giggled at his tiny tool. So frail and weak looking; nothing like
the thick, powerful dick that Shamari possessed.
"Please twerk for me, mommy," he said again.
She looked at him and thought he was such a goddamned
cornball. She gyrated her ass then backed it up until it was flesh
against his chest. He looked as if he wanted to touch it but was
afraid.
"Go ahead. Smack it," she said.
Sure he could slap her ass; after all, he was paying five thousand
dollars to do so.
He gripped her cheeks like he was palming a volleyball. Though
she possessed a nice ass; it wasn't big enough to be compared to a

19

basketball. She bent over right in front of him and smacked the floor with her hands.

He slapped her ass with his penis and she screamed, "Yes, daddy!"

Cornball Dave creamed on her cheeks.

She ran into the bathroom and moments later, she returned with two warm towels. She tossed him one of them.

As he was cleaning himself up, he said, "You know, Ava, I really like you."

She smiled and said, "I like you, too."

He stood and pulled his pants up. "I don't think you understand how much I like you."

"Oh, yeah?"

"Yes. I want to see you more."

"You can see me as much as you want to. You know how to get in touch."

"I want to see you without going through the agency."

"I don't know about that."

"Why?"

"I can't just cut the agency out."

"Look, I don't think you understand. I want to take you away from this life. I don't want you to work for her."

Ava shot him a fake smile. Here was Dave and she was sure he was a nice man. A little too nice, too old and too weird and he was a Captain-Save-A-Ho but she didn't want to be saved—at least not by him. She would let Shamari save her but sure as hell not this weirdo.

"Dave, you're a nice guy."

"But…"

"But, you're trying to take me away from something that I don't want to leave. I love my life. I love making money for myself."

"I want you."

"Why do you want me?"

"You're not judgmental. I know I creep a lot of people out. Nobody understands me."

"What do you want from me?"

"Can't you see I'm lonely? I'm fifty years old. I'm successful, but I have no wife. I have no children. I don't want to grow old alone.

The relationship can be open. You can do what you want to do sexually. I'm not stupid. I know I can't satisfy you."

"You want an arrangement?"

"Yes."

"Not right now. The timing is way off."

"You'll think about it?"

"I will."

He stood and approached her and hugged her. She felt very sorry for him. Everybody deserves love, even creepy-ass Dave.

*****

Inside the Blue Flame strip club Fifty cent and Chris Brown's song "I'm the Man' was playing. Big Ced and Shamari sat in a booth at the back. A waitress named Pinky approached the table then massaged Ced's chest.

"What can I get for you today, daddy?"

Pinky was a tall, light-complexioned woman with a mole beside her mouth and an ample ass.

"Give me a plate of lemon pepper wings, some seasoned fries, and a Bud Light."

Shamari ordered the same and when Pinky had disappeared, Ced said, "I know where the L.A. boys are. The ones that I think might have killed Black."

"Look, bruh, you don't know if they killed Black."

"You're right. But I know that Black had a beef with these clowns and one of these niggas shot me."

"So, is this about your revenge or Black's revenge?"

Pinky dropped the beer and the wings on the table and said, "Let me know if you need anything else, daddy."

Ced smiled. "Thank you, baby." After the waitress disappeared, he said, "I thought Black was your man?"

"He was my man, but I want to make sure that we don't go doing nothing that don't make no sense." He made eye contact with Ced before saying, "I promised his Pops I would find out who did this and that's what I plan to do, but I'm not about to go do something stupid. We need to make sure we got the right people."

21

"How are we 'posed to do that? Black is gone, bruh."
"What makes you so sure that the L.A. dudes were the ones that
killed Black?"
Ced guzzled his beer then burped. "Black got into it with them in
the county jail and one of the L.A. niggas got stabbed."
"Black had a lot of enemies."
"He did." Big Ced flagged Pinky over and ordered another Bud
Light and said, "I just wanted to run it by you. I'm going to find
them with or without you."
There was a long silence and Shamari thought about his friend and
how Black had worked so hard to get him out of prison and how
Black had stuck by him while he was incarcerated. He said, "Let me
run this by TeTe."
"Who?"
"Black's old lady."

B.C., the UPS driver, had just made his fourth stop at a dental laboratory in Powder Springs and was returning to his truck that was parked near the curb when two men approached him. A black man and a white man. He took a step back. This wasn't unusual. People approached him every day about packages, often requesting that he search his truck for an expected package.

The black man said, "Byron Coleman?"
B.C. frowned and wondered how did the man know him. "Yes, that's my name. Did we go to school together?"
"No."
 B.C.'s eyebrows squished together.
"I want to talk to you for a minute," the black man said.
"About what? Who are you?"
"I'm with the FBI and he's with the DEA." The black man pointed to the white man.
B.C. looked around nervously. There was an elderly couple sitting in the car behind the truck fumbling with some paperwork, paying him no mind. B.C. laughed. He thought this had to be some kind of joke until the men flashed their badges.
"What do you want?" B.C. asked. He looked around. The unthinkable was about to happen, he knew that he was going to go to prison for a very long time. He had been catching boxes for Stunna for several years and he had thought he had been getting away with it but here were the Feds standing right in his face. He didn't want to go to prison. He couldn't go to prison. Who would raise his kids and help his girlfriend? He had to make a deal. He would give up Stunna. It was as simple as that.
He stared at the two very serious-looking men that were standing in front of him.
The white man said, "Do you mind if we get on the back of your truck to talk?"
"To talk?"

"We're not going to search. There is no need to search. I know you have a box for Margie Perkins, a made-up name, and that the box contains cocaine. There is really no need for me to search this truck."

B.C. knew he was indeed fucked. B.C. sighed and led them to the truck. They walked to the back of the truck where the boxes were stacked—big boxes, small boxes, and envelopes.

The black man said, "Where is the box?"

B.C. fumbled and found the box and passed it to him. It was a plain brown mirror box, professionally labeled with a yellow sticker that said FRAGILE! HANDLE WITH CARE!

The black man said, "Do you have anything else?"

"No."

"Anything you want to tell us?" the very serious-looking agent asked.

He sighed and said, "The only thing I want to say is that I was just trying to make some extra money. Don't lock me up. I have a family that needs me."

"And what are you willing to do for us? Why should we let you go free? You've been breaking the law."

The white guy looked at Byron and said, "Byron, I know that you've never been in trouble."

B.C. dropped his head and said, "It was a mistake."

"I know it was," the black man said, "and this is what we are going to do. We're going to let you keep working. We didn't notify your job."

"Thanks."

"Whose coke is this?"

"A guy name Stunna. His real name is Alan Green."

The white man said, "Okay, you're going to tell Stunna that the package never arrived. That it was never placed on your truck."

"He's going to know. He's gonna track it."

"Don't worry about that. You just do what we say."

B.C. trembled as he thought about the conversation that he was going to have with Stunna. Stunna was not going to believe him and he was going to slap the fuck out of him because he had just told him that he had possession of the package and now he would have to tell him that he didn't have it. That conversation would not go in his favor.

"I will tell him."

The black man patted B.C. on the back and said, "Calm down. It's going to be okay."

The two agents exited the truck and got into a silver Chevy Impala then sped off.

*****

Jada danced in the mirror to Beyonce's song Sorry. Beyonce's Formation World Tour was coming to Atlanta and she could not wait to go. It was coming in July right around Starr's birthday. Jada planned on surprising her. The phone started to ring and she decided to answer it at the last moment.

"Hello?"

"Jada?"

"Who is this?" Beyonce blasted in the background.

"This is me."

"Who is me?"

"Tank."

"What?"

"It's Tank."

"Tank from Miami?"

"Can we talk?"

"Talk about what?"

"About me and you."

"There is no me and you. Last time I spoke to you, you had a baby on the way and you were pissed that my homeboy was here." Jada remembered the day that she had spoken to Tank. The day that she had fucked Black and Tank had stormed out of her living room.

"Look, I was acting—"

"Like a bitch."

"I was." He laughed then said, "I'm sorry."

"Okay, I accept your apology." She ended the call.

Then the phone rang again and she picked up the phone without looking and said, "Look, Tank, I don't want to talk."

"Wrong person." The person laughed and then said, "It's Barry Daniels."

"And what the fuck do you want?"

"Meet me."

"Are you fucking crazy? I'm not meeting you alone. What do you want from me?"

"I got something for you. Something that is going to benefit the both of us. Can you just meet me?"

Jada thought about the evidence in the phone showing that she had fucked Black. If that evidence got out, it would hurt so many people.

She said, "Give me twenty minutes."

*****

Daniels sat behind a desk in the office. His green and yellow Puma running shoes were resting on the desk. As soon as Jada stepped into the office, he handed her four Beyonce tickets. Backstage passes.

"What the hell?" Jada smiled.

"I'm not as bad as people make me out to be."

"Are these for me?"

"When I called you earlier, I heard Beyonce in the background and I had the tickets. I was going to give them to my wife, but she and her sisters are going to go to the Dallas show, so they are for you."

Jada tried to give him the tickets back but he wouldn't accept them.

He offered her a seat across from him, but she opted to stand. She placed the tickets in her purse.

"Jada, I need your help."

She crossed her arms. "What do you need?"

"Help me get rid of three kilos of coke. We'll split the profit."

"I'm not a trapper."

"But Shamari is."

"He's not going to do that for me."

26

"One thing I know is that you'll help him do anything and he'll help you do anything. Jada, do this for me and you will never hear from me again."

Jada stood silent. She wanted to help this man. She didn't want the secret relationship between her and Black to get out.

"I have one question to ask."

"What is it?"

"Did you kill Black? Or do you know who killed Black?"

"Jada, that's two questions. I'll answer one."

"Did you kill Black?"

"No."

Shamari noticed Jada's nipple impressions showing through her purple sports bra. He was startled when he noticed the three kilos of coke that sat on the coffee table.

He said, "What the hell is going on?"

"This is what I wanted to talk to you about."

"Fresh got you warehousing coke for him? Are you out of your mind? If the police raid this motherfucker, it's over for you."

"This doesn't belong to Fresh."

"Whose shit is this?"

There was a long pause.

"Whose coke is this?" he asked again.

"It's mine."

"So, you're a drug dealer now?" He laughed and said, "Trap Queen Jada."

"Will you be serious?"

"I'll get serious when you tell me why you got three bricks of coke in your house."

She sighed and said, "I was holding it for a friend and he got locked up. He sent word for me to help him sell the shit so he can pay for an attorney." The lie rolled out of her mouth so effortlessly that she almost scared herself.

"Who the fuck is he?"

"You remember Big Papa?"

"Who?"

"The fat dude that you chased away from the hotel room."

"Oh, you still fucking around with his fat ass? I'll take his shit."

"He got murdered while you were on the inside. It belongs to a friend of his."

Shamari bit his top lip. She paced and his eyes followed that ass in those tight skinny jeans. When she turned and faced him, those nipples were peeking at him again.

Her heart drummed. She hated to lie to him, but she couldn't tell
him that she had accepted this coke from Daniels. He would
disown her.

She approached him; her cleavage now inches away. He felt her
body heat.

He glanced at the three packages that lay on the kitchen table,
knowing that they belonged to a stranger. He wondered why he
was there in the first place.

She whispered, "I need your help, Mari. I really, really need you."
She said it seductively though she knew he wasn't some naive
cornball that would fall for anything.

"Whoa. Help doing what?"

She attempted to wrap her arms around him. He shoved her away.
Shamari knew what she wanted from him—she wanted him to
move the coke for her.

"Fresh will help you," Shamari said.

"He can't know about this. I don't have anybody else."

"Why are you doing this, Jada? Why do you feel the need to help
every goddamn drug dealer in Atlanta?"

"It's not like that. It's not like that at all."

"Well, tell me how it is."

Jada plopped down on the chair and said, "I need money, too.
Fresh gives me money and I have the money that you left me, but I
want to get my mother out of the hood. I want to give her a
house." She sighed. "You know how guilty I feel that I live in this
really nice place. Every time I go to Mama's house and see how
broke down and raggedy that house is, I want to help my mama
and I see this as an opportunity to pay down on a house for her. I
can ask Fresh, but you know he has his own shit going on."

Shamari laughed again and it annoyed the hell out of her.

"What are you laughing at?"

He stopped laughing and became serious. "So why me?"

"Because I can tell you anything. You know me. You know I've
always wanted to get Louise out of the hood."

"And you know that once you tell me that story that I will help. I
love your Louise and I would do anything for you."

He approached her and his hands slid up her blouse, caressing her long nipples. She stuck her tongue into his mouth as far as it would go.

*****

Shamari, Big Ced, Jada, and TeTe sat in the den at TeTe's house talking and reminiscing about Black over beer and cheese dip. They had been telling old stories, including the first time that Shamari had met Black.

Fifteen minutes into the conversation, Shamari turned to Ced and said, "Tell her what you told me."
TeTe sat her drink down and her eyes got serious. "Tell me what?"
"I got the drop on the L.A. boys. There is a nigga named Bird and another dude named Low Down. They just moved in a spot out in Alpharetta.
TeTe's nose wrinkled. Black had spoken about Bird, but he had never said anything about Low Down.
Ced interjected, "Black and Bird fought in the county jail and Bird got stabbed."
Jada interrupted. "We all loved him, but we're going to have to let this go. This vigilante attitude is going to get someone hurt." She paused and said, "Everybody in this room is a hustler in some capacity. We like money. We like nice things."
TeTe raised her eyebrows then crossed her legs and said, "What the fuck does that have to do with anything?"
"Black is not coming back."
"You have a bad attitude."
Jada said, "I have a bad attitude because I just stated the obvious?"
TeTe sighed. She was frustrated with Jada's reasoning. She had been taught that if someone takes from you; you take from them. If someone hurts you, you better hurt them. Not this forgive and forget bullshit Jada was preaching.
"So we 'posed to let this shit ride?" TeTe said as she stared at Jada like she was crazy.

"You said for yourself that you didn't think he was killed by gangsters. You want to kill anybody that had a beef with Black?" Jada laughed then downed her drink. "That shit sounds barbaric. You can't go killing people just because you think that they did something."

Ced said, "I know they did it."

"How can you be sure?" Jada said.

Ced turned his nose up at Jada. She was getting on his goddamned nerves.

"You're right. I don't know. But I do know one of the motherfuckers shot me."

"So is this about Black or you? Because if it's about you, I don't know you like that, partna."

Shamari said, "Jada, Ced is right. Black had a beef with them so it's a possibility that they were the people that murdered Black. Look, Black was found on the side of the road just like Big L was."

"Who the hell is Big L?" Jada asked.

TeTe said, "He was Black's flunky. An enforcer that liked having sex with men, but he was very loyal to Black." TeTe was lost in thought as she thought about how similar the two murders were and how perhaps the L.A. boys were, in fact, responsible.

TeTe said, "So where are these boys and how do you know where they are?"

"A girl that I know. Her sister fucks with one of them."

"Another stripper?"

"No." Ced laughed. "Why do you ask that?"

"I was just thinking that maybe you were like Black, always getting all of his information from strippers."

Shamari said, "I'm with Jada on this one. We need to find out more about this before we go killing people for no reason."

TeTe stood and said, "Well, I'm with Ced. Someone has to pay for what they did to my baby and I'm for sure going to get those bitch-ass Detroit boys for what happened to my sister."

*****

Micky was released from the hospital and was doing fine except for a few scars on her face. The doctors had ordered her

31

to rest, but she was rested enough as far as she was concerned. Stunna had called her and told her to meet up with B.C. to get the work that was supposed to have come in. She had spoken with him last night and they both agreed that it would be better if she met with him today since it was late at the time of their conversation. It was shortly after eight p.m. when she arrived on his doorstep. His girlfriend opened the door. A two year old was holding on to her legs, screaming and hollering.

The woman said to the baby, "Mommy is not going anywhere." Micky smiled at B.C.'s baby mother then pinched the baby's chubby cheeks. "When they're that age, they're not letting mommy go anywhere."

The woman shoved a pacifier into the baby's mouth. The baby spat it out. She then hoisted the toddler onto her hip and the crying stopped.

Micky said, "Is B.C. home?"

The woman yelled for B.C. who was in the bedroom in the back. Moments later, he appeared wearing his UPS uniform. The baby mother carried the child into the bedroom. B.C. invited Micky inside the house and offered her a seat.

Micky said, "I didn't know if you were here or not. I didn't see your car outside."

"I don't have it."

"What do you mean?"

B.C. looked at her skeptically. "Stunna took it."

"What? I didn't know that."

"He was pissed that I got it, saying that I was bringing too much attention to myself. Meanwhile, he left me with the eight hundred dollar a month car note."

Micky laughed and said, "Ouch!"

B.C. sat down across from her; kicked off his work boots then asked, "Can I get you anything to drink? We have water and Lime Gatorade."

"No, I have to be going. I just came to get the box so I can roll out, you feel me?"

Without looking at Micky, B.C. said, "I feel you. I have a problem."

"What you mean, you got a problem? Where is the package, bruh?"

"I don't have it."

"What you mean, you don't have it? You told Big Bruh that you had the box. Now where the hell is the box?"

The baby in the backroom started crying and he said, "Hold it down. I don't want my girl to know what I'm talking about."

"She can't hear us, thanks to that loud-ass baby." Micky frowned and said, "So tell me what's going on?"

"I don't have the box."

"What happened?"

"Look, I got on my truck like I usually do, and Stunna called me to make sure everything was okay. I had seen the box so I told him everything was okay. At the end of the day when I was done with my route, I couldn't find it."

"You couldn't find it?" Micky said. "That shit don't even sound right."

B.C. stood and paced. The whining-ass brat was still hollering.

"I don't know, Micky. I think I delivered it to the wrong person. I don't know what happened. I'm so fucked up over this. I don't know what I'm going to do. I know your brother is going to kill me. You're going to have to help me, Micky."

He was making her nervous. She had to calm him down and the brat was making things far worse. She grabbed him by the arm and told him to sit down. He sat but his knee kept jumping. The baby stopped crying.

"Now, tell me. When did you realize that you didn't have the box?"

"Last night after I spoke with you. I was looking for the box like I always do. I was going to take it home, but I didn't see it. That's when I started freaking out. I don't know what was in the box, but I know it had to be a lot of shit in there for Stunna to give me five thousand dollars."

"Damn right it was a lot of shit in there. Five bricks, bruh."

B.C. stood again and started pacing. The baby started crying again. It was as if the baby knew he was in trouble.

Micky said, "Why didn't you call him and let him know as soon as you knew?"

He ran his fingers through his hair and sighed. "You know how your brother is. He's going to hurt me."

"He can be reasonable. You just have to talk to him and I'll make sure that he don't kill you."

He looked at her with pleading eyes and said, "Micky, you've gotta talk to him for me."

She picked up the phone and called Stunna. When he picked up, she said, "Bruh?"

"Yeah?"

Silence. She was trying to think of a better way to tell him. She knew that he was going to be pissed. There was no way to smooth this over. B.C. had fucked up readily.

Stunna yelled into the phone. "What is going on?"

"We have some bad news."

"Bad news?"

"Yeah. It's about B.C."

Stunna was lashing butt-naked B.C. with an extension cord. B.C. was standing in Blue's living room surrounded by six goons—all of whom were dependent on the cocaine making it back to Atlanta to feed their families. Stunna kept lashing him and B.C. hollered as Micky cringed. She felt sorry for the man but she knew there was only so much she could tell her brother.

"Where is my shit?" Stunna said.

"I don't know."

"Tell me where my shit is."

B.C. held onto his welt-filled legs before he plummeted to the floor. The stinging of the cord was just too much for him to handle.

Stunna stood over B.C. "Get your stupid ass up."

B.C. stood and made eye contact with Stunna. "I swear to God, I dunno where your shit is. You've got to believe me."

"Wrong answer." Stunna then pointed a stun gun at B.C.'s dangling balls and shocked the fuck out of him, sending jolts of electricity though the man's whole body, knocking him to the floor. He hollered like a wounded dog. He held his balls and screamed, "I would never take nothing from you. You know I wouldn't. I've been doing this for years and this is the first time that this has happened."

Micky approached Stunna. She attempted to grab his arm and he shoved her back. "Get the hell away from me, sis."

"Listen to him."

Stunna turned to two of the men. "Hold his bitch ass down."

The two men held B.C.'s arms down and his face was forced against the carpet. He squirmed and two more men held his legs until he couldn't move. Stunna lashed his ass cheeks hard three more times.

"I swear to God, Stunna! I swear to you! I don't know where your shit is."

Micky said, "Please, bro. Please let him go."

Stunna took a step back and dropped the cord. "Let him go?"

B.C., still hunched over, was trying to make his way to his feet. When he was finally standing, Stunna ordered the men that had been holding him to exit the room. Blue and Micky remained.

B.C. said, "I would never take from you, man. I know you would kill me. I didn't take it. I swear to God, Stunna."

"I know you didn't take it."

"You believe me?"

"I know you're not that motherfuckin' crazy."

"Why did you beat me so badly?"

"Three reasons. The first reason is because I don't want anybody to think they're going to take a motherfuckin' thang from me. The second reason is because I've lost two hundred thousand dollars because of your dumb ass and the third reason is because I can."

B.C. trembled as he struggled to make eye contact with Stunna.

"I'll make it up, bruh. I promise!"

"Damn right you're going to make it up to me. How much money do you have saved?"

"Twenty thousand."

"My sister is going to follow you home and you're going to give her the money."

"But that's all that I have."

"Do I look like I give a fuck?"

"No."

"Don't worry. I'm going to make sure that you make some more money. After I have made my money back."

"You're still working with me?"

"Why wouldn't I work with you? It was an honest mistake, right?"

"Right," B.C. said, thinking that if Stunna really knew what had happened, there would be no doubt that he would be dead. He was indeed in a fucked-up spot.

*****

Fresh stared at Jada as she lay asleep in his bed. She was wrapped up in a pink, knitted mermaid blanket that she'd bought from home because he always kept it so cold at his place. Even with her hair wrapped in a black silk scarf, she was just beautiful to him. Her full lips slightly parted. He could listen to her breathe all day.

Jada awoke from her sleep. She smiled, revealing dimples that he had never noticed before. She turned onto her side and he climbed into the bed with her. Her ass pressed against his package.
She said, "You were staring. What were you thinking?"
"I was thinking how lucky I am to have someone like you."
She smiled again and then turned and faced him. They stared at each other for a few seconds, their faces only an inch apart when he tried to kiss her but she turned away and he was annoyed.
"What's wrong?"
"Morning breath, baby."
"I don't care. I love you."
Her world froze when she heard those words. She couldn't believe him. She wanted to but the voice in her head told her to be careful.
She stood, yawned, and stretched. His eyes fixated on her body. He wanted to devour her, have his way with her. Her yellow boy shorts crawled up her ass as she stretched and when she caught him stalking her, she said, "You pervert."
He grinned, "You like it."
"I do." She flashed a big smile before running into the bathroom. He trailed her and when she noticed him, he put his hands around her waist right above her hips as she stood in the mirror, holding onto a soft pink toothbrush, applying baking soda toothpaste. She wrestled and tried to break free from him, but couldn't because he was too strong.
She looked up at him. "What are you doing?"
"I want some."
"Want some what?"
He smacked her on her ass and said, "You know what I want."
She laughed and said, "You're in heat this morning."
His manhood throbbed against her ass cheeks.
"You effect me like that."
"Affect, you mean."

"Grammar police."

"Not hardly."

 He released her and she scrubbed her teeth clean before hopping into the shower. He returned to the bedroom and after she showered, she reappeared naked. He smiled then removed his boxer briefs and lay on his back. He stroked his manhood with his hands, hardly able to contain his excitement.

She climbed into the bed then reached for his erect shaft but he blocked her hand. "I want to please you."

He pushed her on her back, her head propped up by a caseless pillow. He spread her legs then nuzzled her inner thighs. She raked his waves with her fingers, anticipating his arrival at her sweet spot. Her juices welled up inside of her.

He took his time, planting a trail of kisses until he finally arrived in the neighborhood of her kitty-kat. Then she started worrying about what he was thinking. She knew she was fresh. She had showered, but she hadn't waxed. She had shaved yesterday, so there was a little stubble. She told herself to calm down. She was freaking out for nothing.

Seconds later, his mouth was on her clit. Yes! He licked her and toyed with it. She felt his gapped teeth and he feasted on her opening. Her juices were cascading onto her inner thighs. Her hands were on his traps, trying to contain him. Trying to tame him. But he savored her body and he was enjoying himself, and this excited her. His index finger plunged deep inside as he ate her. Her clit had become his clit; her body had become his body to do whatever he pleased.

He forced his finger deeper and she said, "Put another one inside me."

Now there were two fingers and his tongue. Goddamn, this man made her feel so good. For a brief moment, she thought about what he had said earlier—that he loved her. She wondered was he just playing.

He turned her over on her stomach and her face was now against that caseless pillow. Now there was one finger in her asshole and one inside her core and his hot tongue on her clit.

"Oh my fuckin' God." She wished this sensation could last forever. "Please penetrate me." She looked over her shoulder then she bit down on that ugly-ass pillow. "Penetrate me," she said again.
"Say please."
Was he serious? Why the fuck was he asking her to beg at this moment. She needed him inside of her right now, but she would play along with his silly-ass games.
"Please, I want you inside me." She couldn't believe he had just made her beg, but whatever.
He pushed his package inside her kitty and his hands held onto her sweaty waist. He plunged deeper and she screamed. He yanked her hair and the sound of his thighs smacking against her ass filled the room. He flipped her over on her back and plunged deeper. His mouth now on her beautiful, erect nipples.
She said, "I want you to cum."
He didn't respond. He kept stroking, and she said, "Please, cum inside me."
He didn't respond. He just kept working. Grinding. Pushing himself inside of her and she said, "What's the matter, daddy? Why won't you cum?"
He removed his tool and he exploded on her stomach.
She flipped onto her stomach, then took possession of his package and devoured all the remaining cum from his shaft. Then she hopped up and ran into the bathroom and returned with two towels; a white one for her, and a yellow one for him.
She tossed him a yellow one and said, "Why didn't you cum inside me?"
"I don't know."
"You afraid that you might get me pregnant?"
"I can't lie. That crossed my mind. Especially now, since I'm on the run."
She smiled, "That's not the worst thing that could happen in the world."
"What are you saying, Jada?" He cleaned his tool with the towel and tossed it in a corner. Then he slid back into his boxer briefs.
"I don't know. I was just thinking it was time for a baby. I know my mom would be happy."
"You want a baby?"

"I'm in my thirties now. I think it's time for one, at least."

He said, "Let me get this case behind me first. I would like more kids."

She smiled then asked, "Did you mean what you had said earlier?"

He ran his fingers through his hair, his mind raced as he wondered what she was speaking of.

"What are you talking about?"

She frowned and said, "Never mind."

"Tell me."

"You said you loved me."

"I meant it."

She smiled and approached him. She hugged him and they kissed.

"I want to make us breakfast after I get out of the shower," she said.

"There is nothing here to eat."

"I'll dash down to Publix to get some food. What do you want to eat?"

"Surprise me."

 She went into the bathroom smiling and showered again. Ten minutes later, she was dressed and she came back into the room. She found him resting on the bed and thought about how comfortable he looked, but in the back of her mind was the thought that he could be taken away from her. He was on the lam. Sometimes she forgot that he was a man that was running. A man who had committed a double homicide. She didn't see that side of him. She never thought of him as a killer. She only saw the kinder, gentler side of him, but she knew that he had another side to him. She also knew that if he didn't have that side to him, she would never have been with him.

He gazed then waved her over and said, "Give me a kiss."

She smiled and leaned into him then pecked him on the lips and said, "I love you, bae, but you need to brush your teeth."

He frowned and said, "Is it that bad?"

"Pretty damned bad."

He laughed and then asked, "Do you need money?"

"No. I can get it but can I drive your car?"

He leaned over to the nightstand and tossed her the keys. "The car is registered in my alias."

"And what name is that?"
"Malcom Boulware."
"That's fine." She laughed and said, "I'll be back in a few."
 "Take your time."

*****

John Clyburn was lying in the bed with a young lady named Willow. He didn't know her last name; all he knew was that she had just had her nineteenth birthday and that she had told him that he was a year older than her grandpa. This revelation would have made most men insecure, but it actually excited John.

He'd found Willow on Backpage and she looked exactly the way he liked them: tall, thin, biracial, and barely legal. He liked the fact that she had a small ass and no hips.
Curves were a sign of womanhood and John never wanted to sleep with women—he wanted girls. He couldn't explain his fetish for young girls but a grown woman's curves didn't arouse him.
Willow arrived at eight last night. Her Backpage ad had said that she was running a special. He called and she said that she would spend the night with him for five hundred dollars. He agreed and she came right over.
They drank five-dollar wine as they talked. She'd shared with him that her father was white and her mother was black. Her father was imprisoned for running a meth lab. She later divulged that her white grandfather had raised her. He had been a drunk but her mother was a crack head, so there was no alternative.
When they were good and drunk, he asked her if was she into anal.
"No."
"But you said I could have my way with you."
"I don't like anal. It hurts."
"What if I give you an extra hundred dollars?"
"And extra two but no rose budding."
"What the hell is that?"
"When a guy tries to turn your asshole inside out."

41

"Even I'm not that perverted."

"Thank God."

After he had his way with her in her tight little ass, they dozed.
The next morning Willow shook John and tried to wake him up.
He looked up at her and said, "Who are you?"

"I'm Willow. I spent the night."

He sat up on the bed. He remembered her now. He remembered
fucking her in the ass until he was exhausted.

She said, "Someone is at your door. They've been knocking for a
while."

"Who is at my door?"

"I don't know."

He made a mad dash to the door before realizing his dick was
swinging and there was some dried semen on his inner thigh—he
was butt naked. He did an about face and grabbed a pair of
pajama pants that were on the bedroom floor. Then he made a
beeline to the door.

"Who is it?"

"It's TeTe."

"Hold on." He disappeared into the bedroom and grabbed an ugly
green V-neck T-shirt out of the closet and slid into it.

Willow said, "Can you please pay me so I can go home?"

"Just one moment."

"No, pay me now."

"Can I talk to my friend for a second?"

Willow folded her arms.

Moments later, John opened the door for TeTe and she barged
right in. "I have to pee. Where is your bathroom?"

John pointed to the bedroom where Willow was. TeTe barged into
the bedroom, walked right passed Willow, and made it to the
bathroom to pee. Five minutes later, she returned to the living
room where John was.

"John, how old is that girl?"

"She's legal."

"How legal?"

"She's over eighteen. So what brings you here?"

"I need you to check out these two guys. Find out everything you
can about them."

"Who?"

"I don't know their names. All I know is nicknames."

"How in the hell can I find out about them if you don't know their names?"

"Their names are Low Down and Bird."

He laughed and said, "So I'm supposed to go in the hood asking about somebody named Low Down and Bird. What am I looking for them for?"

"I think they are the ones that killed Black."

"Black?" John rubbed his chin.

"My ex."

"I honestly thought you killed him."

"Very funny, John."

"Seriously, I thought you knocked him off."

"Well I didn't. I loved him."

"Ok, this Bird and Low Down, what else do you know about them? Any idea how I find these clowns?"

"Black fought one of them in the county jail before he was murdered."

"I'm going to need Black's real name so I can pull his jail record."

"Tyrann Massey. And one of the L.A. boys got stabbed while he was in jail."

John's eyes lit up. "Now we're getting somewhere." He stood and ran into the kitchen to retrieve a pad and a pencil and wrote Black's name down and the relevant dates of the fight."

The bedroom door flung open and Willow appeared struggling with a huge orange overnight bag. She said to John, "Can we handle our business so I can I go?" She set the heavy bag down on the floor.

John said to TeTe, "Excuse me." They disappeared into the bedroom and he paid her. She reappeared in the room and picked up her bag.

"How much did he give you?" TeTe asked.

"Excuse me?" She dug a Marlboro Light from her bag and lit it.

"How much money did he give you?"

John returned to the room and Willow said, "John, who the fuck is she?"

TeTe laughed and said, "Why all the hostility? I just asked a question. I was going to offer you a job."

Willow said, "You? Offer me a job?" Willow laughed.

"Yes. Why is that so hard to believe?"

Willow took a puff from her cigarette then blew out a cloud of smoke. "Doing what?"

"The same thing you're doing with John."

"And what do you think I'm doing with John?"

"Come one, sweetheart, let's not play stupid. What do you have in common with this old man? You're hoeing."

John said, "She can help you. She runs a dating service, matching rich men up with women."

"So why didn't you use her?"

"I'm not rich."

Willow inhaled her Marlboro then blew a smoke ring. "How much does it pay?"

"A lot more than he's paying you."

"You don't know what he paid."

"You're right. That's why I asked. But if you spent the night, he probably got you off Backpage. So you should have made at least a thousand dollars, but I know you didn't get that with him. Five hundred tops."

"I got seven hundred."

"Okay, honey, you overachieved. Do you want to make some real money or not?"

Willow laughed.

TeTe passed her a card and said, "You're a cute girl. Just think about it."

Jada had just left Publix with bacon, fruit juice, a half dozen eggs, and some grits. She was heading back home when her phone rang. It was Fresh. She answered. "Hey, babe."

"How far away are you?"
"About five minutes. Why?"
"Oh, I was about to get in the shower."
"I have your key, remember?"
"Oh yeah." He laughed.
She hung the phone up and thought that it was an odd question but she supposed that he had forgotten that she had taken his car. Five minutes later, she pulled into his garage.
A woman's voice entered the car through the speakers and Jada realized right away that Fresh's phone was connected to the Bluetooth in the car.
The female voice said, "You're always saying that you love me but you don't want to see me. I know you're on the run and you got issues, but I want to be there for you, Fresh. And don't you see that you saying that you love me doesn't make it better? It makes it worse." The voice paused.
Jada was fuming.
The woman continued. "Do you hear me, Fresh? Fresh? Fresh?"
Then there was a dial tone. Fresh opened the door leading to the garage. He stared at Jada for a few moments without saying a word. She guessed that he was gauging how much she had heard. She could sense that he knew something was wrong, but she had decided that she was not going to let him know that she had heard anything.
She smiled and said, "Babe, do you want to help me with the groceries?"
"Of course." He opened the door, retrieved the groceries and then carried them into the house where she fixed him a feast. They talked as usual and he even said that he wanted to meet her

family. After the meal was over, she kissed him and drove home crying.

*****

B.C. was walking back to his truck again when the two Fed agents appeared. They led B.C. to the truck.

The black agent said, "Ok, where is the package?"
B.C. looked confused. "What shipment?"
"Now you're going to pretend to be stupid?"
"Give me the package and we'll be on our way," the white guy said.
B.C. said, "Hey, if you're going to take the work, then take it but you need to protect me, man. The last time I showed up without it, they were going to kill me, man. I swear that man tortured me."
"Where is the box?" the black man asked. "Give me the box."

*****

Shantelle heard the doorbell ring. She opened the door and gasped when she realized that it was Q. "Why are you here?"

She dashed across the room to pick up her cell phone.
Q said calmly, "I'm not going to hurt you. I came to talk."
She set the phone down. She believed him. He'd just gotten out of jail. He surely wouldn't chance going back to prison to harm her. She stepped forward. "What do you want to talk about?"
"Why are you trying to ruin my life?"
Her lips trembled. "How am I going to ruin your life?"
"You know I didn't kill Trey. It was you. I know it was you. It had to be you and I intend to prove it."
"How do you figure that?"
"Look, there was someone that coerced that crazy girl to kill Trey and it wasn't me. All they have on me is that someone had a Houston phone number and they have a rat saying that I wanted Trey dead."
"I never spoke to the police."

"I know it wasn't you. It was a Mexican that got pinched for an unrelated crime and he said he knew about this guy Q who wanted to kill this dude Trey. So when they saw that someone was calling the crazy white bitch from a burner with a Houston number, they thought it was me. But the only problem was the phone signal was in Georgia and that makes me think you knew something about it."

Shantelle was silent.

"You remember you came to Houston, trying to get me to tell Trey not to kill you? He came the very next day and I didn't tell him that I'd seen you because—"

"Because you'd felt guilty that we fucked," she said.

"Maybe. But now that I think back, it was absolutely the wrong thing to do."

"Why would I want Trey dead?"

"Probably because you took his money and you thought he was going to kill you."

She paced and said, "Get out."

"Why did you tell Jada and Starr that I killed Trey?"

"I guess because when I saw you and Starr at Houston's one night and I saw that she was happy, I wanted what she had."

"And so you tried to ruin me by telling her that you think I killed Trey?"

"Let's not act like you didn't want Trey dead."

"At one point I did. I thought that he'd told and I thought that Monte had implicated him. So to make sure he didn't implicate me, I wanted him dead. That's the game we're in. But once I realized I was wrong, I couldn't go through with it."

"Look, Q, I'm sorry about what I did."

"You have me fighting a goddamned case and trying to prove my innocence in a death of a man I loved."

"But you would have killed him if you had to."

"I will kill anybody if I have to...including you."

"Is that why you're here? Are you here to kill me, Q?"

"You think I'm stupid? You think I'm going to kill anybody right now? I'm out on bond."

"So what's next, Q?"

"So are you asking me if I'm going to tell the police what I know?"

She was silent.

Micky was awakened out of her sleep by footsteps in the hallway. She sat up on the edge of her bed. Her heart beating fast and it startled Kelsey, who had been asleep. She sat up on the bed and embraced Micky.

"What's wrong, baby?" Kelsey asked.

"I don't know. I thought I heard something."

"Yeah, I heard it too. It was the sound of someone's footsteps in the hallway." She patted Micky on the back and said, "It's going to be okay. Nobody is going to do anything to you."

Micky faced her and gave her a quick peck on the jaw before standing from the bed. She was wearing blue men's boxer shorts and a wife beater. Her tattooed forearm read TRUELIFE. She picked up her phone from the dresser and saw that she had missed two calls from Stunna.

Kelsey stood and said, "You ever thought about going to counseling?"

Micky turned and faced her and said, "Counseling for what?"

"You've been raped, Mick. You might need to talk to somebody about how you feel. I've been here every day since that happened, and you been waking out of your sleep in a cold sweat. In fear."

"Look, I can handle myself. Don't worry about me. I talked to my brother about it and that's the only person that matters."

"Okay."

Micky's phone buzzed again. It was a text from Stunna.

Stunna: DID YOU GET A CHANCE TO CATCH UP WITH B.C.?

Micky: NO. I CALLED HIM BUT HIS PHONE WAS GOING TO VOICEMAIL.

Stunna: I CALLED HIM TOO.

Micky: I WILL CALL HIM AFTER I TAKE A SHOWER.

Stunna: BET.

Micky fired off a text to Goldie, her other girlfriend, because she hadn't heard from her since the day that she was in the hospital. Micky wasn't sure if Goldie was mad because Stunna had accused her of setting her up. Kelsey approached, peeked over her shoulder and saw the text.

"Why don't you just pick one of us, Mick? Fuck it. Why don't you just fuck with me? Why do you want a dirty-ass stripper?"

Micky shot her a mean look and said, "Now is not the time for it, Kelsey."

"Look, I'm with your brother. Don't you ever think that she might had something to do with you getting raped and them dudes taking the money?"

"As I remember it, you told him where the money was and offered to take them to the stash house. It was you."

"I did it because I love you."

"I know but Goldie loves me too."

"Why do you think she wants you?"

"The same reason you want me. I've got money. I'm no fool."

Kelsey was quiet and they both knew it was true. There was no way Kelsey would entertain Micky if she didn't have money. Kelsey was tall and lean with long legs and she had a bubble butt. She'd never had a problem getting a man's attention.

Kelsey said, "Look, I'm sorry."

"It's okay."

 Kelsey leaned into Micky and they kissed. Micky's hands yanked Kelsey's yellow lace panties down and then pushed her back on the bed. Kelsey removed her bra, revealing small mounds.

Micky leaned into her and kissed her neck, her hands gripping her ass before diving head first between her legs. Her tongue wrestled with her clitoris and Micky savored it. Micky then licked the entrance. Her tongue going in and out of Kelsey's tunnel before Kelsey hopped on top of her. Micky's leg was between Kelsey's legs and Kelsey rode her until the phone rang. Micky tossed Kelsey aside and ran over to the phone and Kelsey frowned. Micky thought it might be Goldie. She hadn't heard from her since the rape. The phone said B.C.

"Hello?"

"It's B.C."

"What's up, bruh? Is everything good?"

"No. I don't have the work."

"What are you talking about?"

"Man, can we meet up?" B.C. asked.
"Yeah. Where?"
"Come to my house. I took the day off."
"Okay, I'll see you in an hour," Micky said.

*****

When Micky arrived at B.C.'s home, she heard that crying-ass baby again. She knocked on the door and B.C.'s baby mama opened the door with the spoiled brat holding on to her leg like before. Micky smiled and asked if B.C. was home. The woman invited her in. The brat was standing there shirtless, wearing a pamper exposed and herniated belly button with her arms outstretched for mommy to pick her up. The woman hoisted the baby up on her waist like before as Micky stood there.

"Where is B.C.?"
"He's not here."
"What do you mean he's not here? I just spoke with him and he told me to come right over. Where is he?"
The woman passed Micky a note—a sheet of loose leaf paper with scribblings from a black marker.
Micky read the note: I'M SO SORRY BUT I DON'T HAVE THE PACKAGE AND THERE IS NO WAY I CAN FACE STUNNA. I KNOW HE WILL KILL ME. THE TRUTH IS THE FEDS CAME TO SEE ME ON MY ROUTE AND THEY KNEW ALL ABOUT THE PACKAGE. I GAVE IT TO THEM, BUT I DIDN'T TELL THEM SHIT.
Micky looked at the baby mama, who was still rocking the baby, trying to calm her whining ass down.
"Call B.C."
"You want his number?"
"No, I want you to call him."
The woman pulled an iPhone from her pocket and called him then passed the phone to Micky.
B.C. answered and asked, "Is she gone?"
"No, I'm still right here, motherfucker."
"Look, Mick, I'm sorry that happened."

51

"So the Feds took it, huh?"
"Yes, I swear to God, Mick."
"And they didn't arrest you?"
"I don't know why they didn't arrest me."
"So all that bullshit about you misplacing the package was a lie?
They took the first one too?"
"Yes."
"You know Stunna is not going to like this."
"I know. It's the truth."
"I mean, why didn't you tell him that the Feds were investigating
him?"
"I don't know, Mick. I swear to God, Mick, I didn't tell them shit."
"But you don't know the names of the officers?"
"I didn't ask."
"You know this shit sounds fishy?"
"I know, but it was one black one and a white one. A big black
dude with a beard."
"That's half of Atlanta."
"Where are you?"
He hung up the phone. Micky tried to call him back but he didn't
pick up. She dialed Stunna who picked up on the first ring.
"What's up?"
"B.C. says he's been pinched. Said that the Feds took the package.
I'll tell you all about it."

*****

Stunna opened the door, invited Starr in, and then led her to
his balcony before offering her food and drinks. She declined.

"So what brings you over? I'm surprised," Stunna asked.
"I just wanted to thank you for coming over the other day and
hearing me out."
"That's the least I can do."
She smiled and she noticed that he wasn't quite himself. He was
more reserved than usual.
"What's wrong?"
"Nothing to concern yourself with."

"Look, you were there for me and I want to be there for you."
"Really, it's nothing, some losses." He poured himself a glass of
Ciroc.
"What kind of losses?"
"You know how the game can be?"
"Yeah, I know. I used to listen to Trey all the time when he'd lose.
He'd mope around the house for a few days before realizing that
he had to get off his ass."
Stunna grinned then took her hand in his and said, "You better
believe I ain't been sitting on my ass."
"How much did you lose?"
"Shit, including the money that Micky lost, I've lost about twenty
kilos and a couple of hundred thousand dollars."
"Whoa."
"I know. I don't really care about the losses."
"You don't care about the losses? Damn, that's almost a million
dollars. I was going to ask if you wanted to borrow some money,
but since you can stand a million-dollar loss and not care, I'm
going to keep my little coins to myself." She laughed.
"No, I didn't mean it like that." He laughed then he smiled and
took hold of her hand again and said, "Were you serious about
what you said?"
"About what?"
"That you would help me out."
"Yes."
"I don't need it, but it is always nice to know that you got my
back."
"Of course."
"So what about me and you?"
"What about us?"
"I like you."
"I like you, too."
"So what's the hold up?"
"Ah, I don't know."
"Starr, I really like you and I know you want better for your son
and I don't blame you. I want the best for my kids, but we are who
we are."
"Meaning?"

"Meaning you can't help who you like. You are attracted to guys like me and there is nothing wrong with that."

She was silent.

"What are you thinking?"

She turned from his gaze and started people watching before turning back to him to make eye contact. "You know what? You're right."

"I know I am."

"So what's next for you?"

"I don't know. I have to find someone around here who has what I need because I keep losing my money."

"How did you lose it?"

"UPS."

"You're sending your shit through UPS?"

"Yeah."

"Trey never trusted UPS. He always said that was a quick way to go to jail."

"How'd he do it?"

"He just put someone on the road and they brought it back for him."

"I don't think I can do that from Cali. Besides UPS has worked for me for a long time. I had a driver and he would bring me the work but the last couple of times, the work hasn't been showing up. I don't know if they are on to me or what, but I can't keep losing money. You feel me?"

"Yes. A million dollars? I would be crying right now. I can ask Jada's ex if he could help you. He's a good dude. A stand-up dude. He was partners with Black."

"Where is he from?"

"Atlanta."

"What's his name?"

"Shamari?"

"Describe him."

"Medium height, hair is now twisted. Kind of built. Light-skinned dude."

"I don't know him. You think he can get me what I need?"

"I don't know."

"Hey, it's worth a try."

When Shamari gave Jada the money for the three kilos, Jada was wearing a pink backless dress that she'd gotten from an Instagram boutique, and she looked astonishing. He noticed it right away and he said, "So are you going out with your boy tonight?"

"No, I'm actually taking my mom out."

He looked around then he asked, "When was the last time you seen Fresh?"

"I saw him this morning."

"Oh, I was trying to call him and his phone was going to voicemail."

He eyeballed Jada. "So what's up?"

"I need a favor."

He looked at her skeptically then said, "I'm not moving no more coke for you."

"Starr has been seeing this dude named Stunna. I know him; Black knew him."

"So where is this going?"

"He's looking for work."

"Why don't you introduce him to Fresh?"

"I want you to make the money. Plus, he's from Atlanta and you're from Atlanta. I don't know how this dude would feel about some dude coming to his city serving him. Stunna has a lot of influence around here."

"So you want me to meet him?"

"Yeah."

"Ok. He's cool?"

"Yes."

"How do you know?"

"He was at Black's funeral."

"Hell, every D-boy in Atlanta was at Black's funeral. So when does he want to meet?"

"Now, if you can."

"Are you going with me?"
She huffed and said, "I don't want to go, but I'll go if it will make you happy."
"It's not a point of me being happy. You're the one that is vouching for the nigga. So you need to be there."
"Okay."
"So who all is going to be there?"
"I guess me and you and Stunna and Starr."
"Set it up."
Jada called Starr and they decided to meet at Jada's place.

*****

The first thing Shamari thought was that this nigga was just as flashy, if not flashier, than Black. He reminded him of Black—a dark-skinned brother with gold fronts on the bottom. The second thing he thought was what in the hell was he doing with Starr. He definitely didn't seem like her type.

Starr had dated hustlers just like her friends Jada and Lani but Starr always dated the clean-cut type of guy. But now she was with some guy with this larger-than-life D-Boy persona.
He approached Shamari with his hand out and said, "I'm Alan but my friends call me Stunna."
"Mari."
"I hear you were a friend of Black's."
"Yeah."
"Were you at the funeral?"
"Yeah.
"Me too." Stunna sighed. "Me and Black did a little business together a few times but we could never get the numbers right. He always wanted to come out on top. Never wanted to give me a break. But we were cool. I used to gamble with him. How do you know Black?"
"Met him in State prison."
"Ok."
"Me and Jada will be in the den while y'all discuss whatever you are going to discuss," Starr said.

After the girls left, Shamari and Stunna sat on opposite ends of the
sofa.
"Look, I'm looking for some white girl, lots of it," Stunna said.
Shamari said, "Before we get started talking about this, let me tell
you this."
Stunna's eyes grew as he waited on Shamari.
"I just got out of the Feds," Shamari said.
"What the hell? Damn, bruh, I'm glad you told me that."
"I was in there for almost a year, before one of the witness
recanted his statements and I got immediate release."
Stunna said, "I appreciate you telling me that. Most dudes
wouldn't have told me a damn thing. They would have just wanted
the money."
"I'm not like most dudes."
"My lawyer said that they might want to indict me again."
"You know what, Shamari? Fuck that! I want to do business with
you. You seem like a stand-up dude."
"What were you looking to get?"
"A few bricks, if you don't kill me on the number."
"We'll work something out."
"I want to start off with one and if I like it. I'll get ten."
The men shook hands.

*****

Brooke burst into Starr's office to tell her that Q was there.
Starr entered her show room and saw Q standing there playing
with his phone. There was a customer that was in the far
corner looking at a sofa.

Starr approached Q and said, "Why are you here?"
He threw his hands up and laughed. "I didn't come for trouble. I
just need five minutes of your time."
Brooke said, "Do you want me to call the police?"
"Five minutes and I promise I'll never bother you again."
Starr huffed and said, "Follow me."
She led Q to the back office. When the door closed, Starr looked at
her watch. "It's two forty-five. You have until two fifty."

"I ain't kill Trey."

"I know."

"I had nothing to do with Trey's murder. I will admit that I wanted him dead at one time, but only because it's part of the game. When I found out that Trey didn't talk, I didn't want him dead. The people I worked for thought he was talking, so they wanted him dead. I thought I told you this."

Starr said, "Cut the bullshit. If they wanted him dead, then you wanted him dead."

"But there was no way I was going to kill him. I didn't want any part of that."

"And I'm supposed to believe you?"

"I don't care what you believe."

"Well then, why are you here?"

She glanced at the watch. Two minutes had passed.

"Just to tell you I didn't do it."

"Okay. Well, how do we explain that there was a Houston phone number texting the girl encouraging her to do it?"

"I can't explain it. All I can say is it wasn't me."

"Yeah, I probably shouldn't be telling you about this number because if you had Trey killed, you should rot in hell."

"I already knew about the Houston phone number. I learned it from my attorney." He looked at her with very sincere eyes and said, "It wasn't me."

"We don't know that, do we?" She looked at the clock. "You have two minutes."

"I'm good, ma. I don't need two minutes."

"How did you get out? Did your little girlfriend get you out?"

"I've said all I'm going to say."

He turned to walk away and she said, "Quentin, don't bring your ass up in my place of business again. Ever."

Ava was whisking green tea in a cup when the doorbell rang. She opened the door for Shamari. She offered him some and he declined.

She said, "So what brings you over?"
"I thought about what you said."
Her skin tingled at the sight of this man.
"You know, about if I wanted you to stop working that I should claim you? And you're right. I have no right to ask you to stop doing anything if I don't claim you or want to be with you."
"So you came all the way over here to tell me I'm right?"
"I want you." He paused. "I don't want you sleeping with men for money. Unless it's me."
She laughed. "So you're going to take care of me?"
"If I need to."
"I'm just kidding, Shamari. I'm not some chick that's going to sit on my ass and spend your money. I've done that before when I was younger and I like a man with money, but I'm not a lazy chick."
He flashed a toothy grin. "I like that."
"So, what made you come to this conclusion?" she asked.
"I like you, and I don't want anyone else to have you."
"It's always nice to feel wanted. Honestly, I thought that you were going to get back with Jada."
"She has her man."
"She still likes you." She paused. "I don't share. But if she wanted you, I guess we wouldn't be having this conversation."
"What are you asking me?"
"Am I your backup plan cuz' shit didn't work out with Jada?"
"Of course not."
"Do you love Jada?"
"Always will, I can't change history. I've been through a lot with her." He paused. "Y'all still hang out?"
"Not recently. I don't know about Jada. I like her and I think we are a lot alike but I don't know if she likes me."

"Jada is kind of funny like that. It takes a while for her to warm up
to people but when she's your friend, she's very loyal."
"I get that from her."
"So it's official between us?"
"As far as I'm concerned, but I don't think I'll be hanging out with
Jada."
"I don't care about that." He made his way over to her side of the
room and slid his hands into her shirt, gripping her breasts.
She frowned. "What are you doing, horndog?"
He made a sad face. "So I can't have any?"
"Not right now. But later for sure. Let's put on a show for the guys
in the next building."
"You freak, you."
"You like it."
"Love it."

*****

A day earlier Stunna had purchased some product from
Shamari. Shamari consigned him and Stunna had gotten rid of
the product. He called Shamari to pick up his money and
invited him for a drink at Wet Willies. Micky came along with
Kelsey. Over frozen drinks they discussed business. Shamari
and Stunna ordered Call A Cabs, a cherry and strawberry
slushie with alcohol and the women ordered Sex on the Beach.

Stunna introduced Micky to Shamari "She knew Black." Then he
turned to Micky and said, "Shamari was one of Black's best
friends."
"You're from Atlanta?"
"Born and raised."
"Good to meet you."
"His girl Jada is a friend of Starr's."
"My ex girl."
Micky said, "I met Jada. How did you let that fine-ass woman get
away from you? I would have done anything I had to do to keep
her."
"A dildo and a tongue is not going to keep a woman."

61

They all laughed. He'd had a friend named Duke whose cousin was a dyke. She had set him and Duke up. He couldn't help but think about Duke.

Shamari said, "So what did you think of the product?"

"It was fire. Got anymore?"

"For sho."

"I just wanted you to meet my sister because sometimes I'll send her to meet up with you."

"It's all love, brother."

Micky said, "I like him. He's real. I can tell."

"I try to be."

"I want to order ten."

"However many you need, I got them."

Micky's phone rang but she didn't answer.

Stunna said, "Who was that?"

"Detective."

Shamari's eyes got big.

"Micky got raped a few weeks ago."

Shamari looked at Micky and wondered who in the hell would want to rape her. Having sex with her would be like fucking a man. Who could even get an erection with her? He'd concluded that the dude that screwed her had to be gay and secretly wanted a guy. Micky dropped her head. She was ashamed it had happened. No matter how much she pretended to be tough, she was no match for a man and she knew it.

"Sorry it happened."

Stunna said, "Don't be sorry for us. Be sorry for him."

"You know who did it?"

"Not yet." Micky said.

Stunna said to Micky. "Have you heard from that bitch Goldie?"

"Every day." Micky lied.

"I think she had something to do with it. I have a gut feeling."

Kelsey said to Stunna. "Say it again. I don't trust her."

*****

Jada was listening to Rihanna's Pandora station as she brushed her teeth, preparing to head to the gym, when the doorbell rang. She ran through the house, naked, until she arrived at the door. She peeked through the peephole and saw a beautiful, brown, doll-faced woman with a button nose and penciled eyebrows. Jada had never seen the woman and figured that she had something for sale or maybe the bitch was a Jehovah's Witness; some people would usually pop on trap music with vulgar lyrics and that would run them away. She decided against that and opened the door as far as the chain allowed. She peeked around the edge of the door.

She said, "Yes. How can I help you?"
"I'm looking for Jada."
"And who are you?"
"Tammy."
"Tammy who?"
"We have mutual friends. I just need a moment of your time."
"Let me slip into my robe first."
Jada threw on a robe, lowered the volume on the music, and opened the door. This Tammy bitch was standing there with a little boy. He looked to be about five years old.
"Yes, can I help you?"
"Can I come in for a moment?"
"First, before I invite you in, let me ask, who do we know in common?"
"Desmond."
"Fresh?"
"Yes."
Jada sized the woman up and she really couldn't hate on the bitch. Except for those etch-a-sketch-ass eyebrows, she was cute. She thought this was some woman that Fresh had been fucking around with so she invited her in.
"Look, I really didn't want to barge in your house like this, but I wanted to talk to you, woman to woman." She handed the child a Nintendo DS and said, "Play with this while I speak with Miss Jada."
The child smiled, happy that he was able to play with his game.
"Who are you? Are you a girlfriend of his?"

"I'm the baby mama."
Jada examined the kid; he was the spitting image of Fresh.
"So you came from Houston?"
"Yes."
"How did you find me?"
"I have my ways. I'm a woman. You know we got our intuitions."
Jada nodded her head. She was furious. Who was this bitch to
barge up in her house and confront her about Fresh? If it wasn't
for the poor innocent child looking so cute playing his video game,
she would have beat the brakes off this ho.
"So let me guess, you and Fresh are still seeing each other."
"We never stopped."
"He lied."
"He always lies."
Jada said, "Maybe you're lying."
"I'm not."
The little boy was pressing the controllers on his game, yelling,
"Go, go, go."
Tammy said, "Hold it down or I'm going to take the game."
"Okay, mommy."
Tammy said to Jada, "We've had our ups and downs and we've
been off and on for years, but I have time invested in this man."
"I see."
There was a ring on her engagement finger.
"Yes, we're engaged."
"How long?"
"For a couple of years."
Jada sighed. She wanted to cry because she knew that this woman
was right. This was absolutely the voice that she had heard coming
through the speakers.
"I'm sorry, Jada."
"It's not your fault."
"I didn't want to come here."
"So why did you?"
"I want to fight for what's mine. I want to fight for my family."
Jada thought back to a conversation that she had with Fresh and
he'd said that there was no way he could be with his baby mother.
All lies.

"See, Jada, he needed you."
"What?"
"Well, you know the predicament he's in. He needed someone to help him."
Jada smiled politely. She felt like a goddamned fool. She said, "Tammy, is there anything else that you want to tell me?"
"No."
"Okay."
"Well, I have to be going," Tammy said.
Tammy grabbed the child and led him to the front door. Just before Tammy reached the door, she turned to Jada and said, "I'm sorry."
Jada just nodded and when the door closed, Jada said
"How could I have been such a goddamned fool?" she cried to herself.

Jada was on all fours and Fresh was forcing every inch of his eight-inch penis inside her walls. He was snatching her new Malaysian hair extensions and slamming her head against the headboard. Her ass was elevated as he was slapping it. Jada was enjoying the session and trying to keep her mind off his baby mama.

She had made up her mind that Fresh wasn't for her. She hadn't said anything to him about the meeting with Tammy, and she doubted that he knew about it. There was nothing unusual about how Fresh was acting. He didn't act any different than before. Nothing to suggest that he had known a meeting had taken place. So when he came over, he kissed her, and shortly afterwards, he wound up with his hands between her legs. Then he removed her jeans, her panties, and her bra and now, her ass was in the air and he was pounding her relentlessly.

She flipped on her back and held her legs open. He was gripping her ankles as he plunged deep inside her love hole. He nibbled her neck and circled her earlobe with his tongue and she was thinking about Tammy. Jada knew she didn't want him to cum inside her anymore.

She said, "I want you to pull out when you cum."

"Huh?" He stopped.

She knew she wasn't making any sense. She wanted him but didn't want him.

"I love you, Jada."

"Don't say that."

"It's true."

"It's not true. Don't say that."

He pulled out, his member still stiff. She sat up on the bed, clenched the pillow, and held it in her lap. She didn't know why she covered herself. This man had seen her body plenty of times. He had just been inside her a few seconds ago, but this move was consistent with her mood.

"What's the matter?" he asked.
"Nothing."
"Something is wrong. I can tell."
"Why do you say that?"
"Just the other day, you were asking me to cum inside you, and now you're saying not to."
"I want to be a wife, not a baby mama."
"Okay."
"I'm getting on the pill."
"Good idea."
She assaulted him with the pillow and said, "Oh, you want me to be on the pill, huh? I'm not good enough to have your baby? You're a fuck boy, Fresh."
"Oh my God, here we are with this fuck-boy bullshit." He laughed and his laugh annoyed her. He picked the pillow up and said, "Look, you were just saying that you wanted to be a wife and not a baby mama then you said that you were getting on the pill and I just simply said that it was a good idea."
She knew that what she was saying didn't make a whole lot of sense but she was hurting.
He slid into his boxers and sat on the edge of the bed. "Why didn't you want me to say that I loved you?"
"It's because you don't."
He stood and she checked out the bulge in his underwear, wishing that she could have that dick without him being attached to it.
"I do love you."
"Fresh, cut the bullshit. You love Tammy and you know it."
He laughed and said, "What?"
"Tammy...um your baby mama?"
"What are you talking about?"
"Nothing."
"You've been in my phone."
"Your phone is locked."
"What does that mean to a snooping-ass chick?"
"Fuck-boy Fresh. That's what your new name is."
"Do you know any other word?"
"Can you act any other way?"
"Whatever."

"I'm sorry for calling you out by your name." She stood and slid into a pair of grey gym shorts.

"What's wrong with you?"

"Look, your baby mama came over yesterday—with your son."

"And that's why you're tripping? What did she tell you?"

"She said that you and her were basically together and you were using me."

"You believe that?"

Jada covered her head. Dudes were so predictable and it was just a matter of time before he said, SHE'S JUST MAD CUZ SHE AIN'T GOT WHAT YOU HAVE.

"Why shouldn't I believe her? She has your son and that woman didn't come all the way from Houston unless you were misleading her."

"I ain't been misleading nobody. She's just mad cuz she ain't got what you have."

"Please save that tired line for some other dumb-ass bitch because Louise ain't raise no fool."

"Who?"

"You see, you would have known that if you met my mama, but you didn't want to and now I know why."

"We can go to meet your mama right now if you want."

"What I want you to do right now is call your baby mama and tell her that you ain't with her."

"Huh?"

"Call your baby mama right now and tell her that you are with me."

"I can't do that. It's more complicated than that."

"Whatever, Fresh."

"Jada, if I do that, she won't bring my son to see me and when I do turn myself in, she definitely won't bring him to see me. That would kill me, Jada."

"Just know that you're playing a dangerous game."

"I love you, Jada."

"Why don't you just get the hell out, Fresh? I ain't got time for your bullshit."

*****

Jada and Starr sat on the balcony and sipped margaritas while watching the sunset. Jada sipped her drink and said, "I want to tell you a secret that I haven't told anyone."

Starr set her drink down and said, "This sounds heavy. What's going on?"

Jada's face became serious and she said, "You have to promise not to tell anyone."

"I promise." Starr said as she stared at her best friend and wondered what could she possibly want to tell her that she hadn't shared with her already. They shared everything between each other.

Jada was silent.

"I'm waiting."

"Look, I know you're going to think bad of me, Starr. That's the thing. You can be so judgmental sometimes and I listen to you without judging."

Starr sighed and said, "You're right, Jada. I promise I won't judge you. Now what happened?"

Jada turned from Starr's gaze. "I fucked Black."

"Whoa," Starr said. "I was not expecting that."

"Yeah, I know. I'm not proud of it."

"How did that happen?"

"I felt kind of vulnerable one day and he came by."

"Came by? What did he come by for?"

"I don't remember, maybe to leave some money for Shamari."

"And one thing just led to another. Bryson Tiller was playing and I was horny. I don't make no excuses, I was wrong. I know I was."

Starr looked at Jada, who was avoiding eye contact with her. She knew that Jada felt horrible. Even in death, Lani was her best friend and there were some lines that she personally would not cross.

Starr took Jada's hand and held it. "It's over. You can't punish yourself for that."

Jada said, "So you don't think bad of me?"

"You made a mistake. You admitted it. Move on."

"What about Lani?"

"If Lani was here, would you have done it?"

"Hell no."

"Okay, it was a mistake, move on."

Jada smiled and thought that it had not been a mistake. She had wanted to fuck Black that night, but if Lani had been living, there was no way that she would have gone through with it.

"You seemed relieved."

"I am. I am so happy that I can tell you anything. Hypothetically, what if this got out? How do you think Shamari would react?" Jada asked.

"Shouldn't you be worried about Fresh? He's your man."

"Fuck Fresh. I'm pissed at him right now, but I'll tell you about that later. Besides Shamari and Black were close."

"How do I think Shamari would react?"

"Yeah."

"This can't get out."

"I know."

Starr released her hands and said, "Don't tell anyone this. You'll hurt a lot of people if they knew this, including Fresh. It would probably devastate Shamari, since he thought that you had fucked Black before."

"I know."

"Really, Jada. Do not tell anyone."

*****

Jada obstructed the doorway as Fresh stood outside on the porch with his thumbs on the loops of his pockets, like a kid.

They stared at one another for a moment before she invited him in.

When the door was closed he said, "Look, I'm sorry."

"Stop it right now. There is no need to apologize."

"I feel the need to."

"Well, you don't."

"Jada, why are you being so difficult?"

"I'm being difficult?" She laughed and then said, "You don't even want to see me being difficult."

"Hey, Jada, I want to be with you. I want to get married."

"Cut the bullshit, Fresh. I don't want to hear it."

"It's not bullshit."

"Just imagine how I felt when I heard you talking to that bitch when I was in your car."

"What are you talking about?"

"The day I drove your car to Publix. Your phone was connected to your Bluetooth and when I pulled back inside your garage, I heard you tell her you love her."

Fresh looked away before saying, "It's my son's mom, Of course I'm going to always love her, but I'm not in love with her. I ain't going to lie. I said it."

"There is no need to lie. I heard it and I saw the engagement ring."

"She's had that ring for years. I want you and not her. I have to play this little game, and if I don't play the game, I don't get to see my son. Please understand."

"I understand and I'm not upset. I was mad as fuck in the beginning because I thought that you meant what you said. I told my mom about you and she wanted to meet you and I was so open about the possibility of having a husband and my own family."

"And we can still have that—after I surrender and beat the case. When I get out, we can go from there."

"Look, Fresh, you do you and I'm going to do me."

"What is that supposed to mean?"

"It means that I'm over whatever it is we were supposed to have. I like you and I might even fuck you, but that's where it's going to stop. There is no point in me thinking that we can be more than fuck-buddies."

"I see. I guess I can take my gift with me back to the dealership."

"What gift? The dealership?"

Jada ran to the window. There was a silver BMW X 6 wrapped in a red bow. "What the fuck?"

"Yeah, it's for you."

She giggled. "Who buys a car for someone while they're on the run?"

"I do."

"I've tricked for money before, but you can't buy me. I don't think you understand. I thought what we had was real."

"Take the car."
"Take it back to the dealership."

Jada met Barry Daniels in a Kroger's parking lot in Riverdale, Georgia. She hopped into the car with him.

"So what did you decide to do?"
"Look, what do you want me to do?"
"Tell me about the dope."
"I have no idea what you're talking about."
"You don't have to lie. Nobody is going to get arrested."
"I'm supposed to believe you? I know you killed Black,
"motherfucker."
"Nobody is going to get hurt."
"How do I know that?"
"Well, nobody is going to get hurt unless I feel like my life is in danger."
"Fresh is about to send this girl named Shantelle to Houston to pick up some shit. I'll give you have her cell phone number. Maybe you can bug it or something. She's going to bring back some big shit. Lots of it. I don't know, maybe thirty kilos."
"That's it? Look, I know these dudes are cartel connected. I need to know where the big shit is."
"This is it."
"When and where is this going down?"
"She's going to go down to Houston on Saturday and she'll be back on Monday."
"I need exact dates."
"What's in this for me?"
"I'll destroy this phone." Barry Daniels waved Black's Iphone.
"I need some cash, bruh. I got bills and shit to pay too."
"What kind of money?"
"I don't know, maybe thirty thousand."
"What?"
"Yeah. I need some money too. I know you're going to get thirty kilos of coke."

"Jada, I'll give you twenty-five thousand dollars as soon as you give me the information."
"Look, nobody is to know about this. You realize that I will get murdered if they find out I'm doing this. These are gangsters."
"I'll make sure this don't come back to you."
She smiled and said, "And make sure you get rid of that phone."
"Don't worry. Nobody will find out about your little rendezvous."
She smiled. "Perfect."

*****

TeTe's private investigator, John, had some news that he wanted to share about the L.A. boys. Jada and Shamari met him at TeTe's house for Sangrias.

John said, "The good news is I found the L.A. boys. I know where they are, but the bad news, well its good news for them, is that they didn't kill Black."
TeTe set her drink down and said, "How the fuck do you know this?"
"Well, they didn't kill him because they were still locked up when Black got out and they were locked up on the day that he got murdered. So it couldn't have been them."
Shamari said to John, "Who the fuck was it then?"
TeTe said, "I have a feeling that it was Barry Daniels. I have a feeling he had something to do with it."
John said, "I contacted one of my friends that I used to work with on the police force. He's in the FBI and he didn't know Daniels but there was another agent named Elaine Garcia that said that he wasn't well liked around the office but was still a good agent. Maybe you should just tell Elaine what you believe."
"Absolutely not," TeTe said. "That opens up a whole 'nother can of worms. Then we gotta tell them Black was dealing and then they might look at my ass and you know I ain't legit. Fuck that."
"TeTe is right," Shamari said.
"So, what are you going to do? You can't go kill the man based on something that you have no proof of."
"Wanna bet?" TeTe said.

"Look," Shamari said, "I want to get the person that did this to Black just as bad as anybody else, but there is no way I'm going to be a part of that shit."

"I'll do it myself then."

The room was quiet. There was no doubt in anybody's mind that TeTe had the capability to do it.

*****

Shantelle said to Jada, "You ever do something that you regret?"

Jada thought about how she had fucked Black and how even though it was great sex, she wished she hadn't done it. He was the only person that she had ever regretted fucking and the sex had turned out to be mind-blowing.

"Everyone has done things that they have regretted, especially me."

Shantelle huffed then avoided Jada's eyes.

"What did you do, Shantelle? You can tell me."

"I slept with Q."

"What?"

"Yes, I fucked Q. It was around the time that I had taken the money from Trey. I went down to Houston and I told him what I had did and asked him if he would talk to Trey and ask him not to hurt me. At the time, I'd had half of the money and I was going to give it back."

Jada said, "So you slept with Q? I thought you were about to say that you had slept with him recently."

"No, this was before he had gotten with Starr."

"Okay, so you fucked him no big deal."

"That's not all."

"What?"

"I don't really know if Q had something to do with Trey's murder. I suspected that he did because he had come to me wanting him dead but I'm not sure."

"Ok, so what makes you not sure now?"

"I was never completely sure, but I thought it was a possibility."

"And you don't think it's a possibility now?"

"I think it's still possible, but I am not absolutely sure." Shantelle stood and paced. "Jada, I did some real foul shit. I saw Q and Starr out and they seemed like they were enjoying themselves and I was jealous because you know my history with Starr. Even when I was with Trey, I could tell that he liked her and he wanted to be with her. And when I saw you at the mall, I saw it as an opportunity to plant a seed that he might not be what she thinks he is."

"So you were hating?"

"I wasn't hating."

Jada rolled her eyes at Shantelle. "You see someone happy with someone else living their life and you become jealous. That's called hating ho'"

"Jada, I'm sorry. I hate that I did this and I'll tell Starr if you want me to."

"No, I kind of figured your ass was lying because you gave two separate accounts about what happened. One time you said some Mexicans threw you in a van, but when you and I talked the first time you said you met Q at a restaurant."

"You picked up on that?"

"I pick up on everything."

"So why didn't you say something?"

"Because I don't particularly like Q's ass. So I didn't give a fuck if you changed your story as long as the basis of the story was true." Jada was thinking that she had to have Shantelle make the run for Fresh so Barry Daniels could get what he wanted. Otherwise, she would have whopped Shantelle's hoeing ass right there on the spot.

"Starr can't know this," Jada said.

"You know I can't make a run for Fresh anymore because Q will find out. Jada, he's going to have me killed. He thinks that I told on him but I never went to the cops on him. I only told you and Starr what I thought was a possibility."

"Yeah, you told us it was a possibility, but you presented the shit like it was a fact. Let's keep the story straight."

Shantelle frowned and said, "Jada, you're mad at me?"

"No, I'm not mad, but I just want you to keep the story straight."

"Yeah, you're right. But I think he's going to try to kill me."

"I won't let that happen and I need you to make one run for Fresh."
"But what about Q? Won't he find out?"
"Don't worry about Q. I'll handle Fresh."

Starr picked up the frosty green buds from the coffee table when she walked into Jada's home. "Is this Fresh's?"

"No, it's mine."

"I didn't know you smoked."

"I don't. I used to and I'm debating about whether I should smoke it or not."

"Don't do it." Starr sat down on an end chair and laid the buds back on the table.

"I'm so fucking stressed."

"Girl, don't let that shit about Black stress you out. Black is gone and he ain't coming back. Don't worry about it."

"I didn't tell you everything."

Starr's eyes grew. "What else do you have to tell me? What did you leave out?"

"There is somebody else that knows that I fucked Black."

"Jada." Starr gave her the side eye. "I told you not to tell anyone."

"This dude knew before I told you."

"That dude Tank?"

"No."

"Before Black died, he was working with a crooked FBI agent. The man would take drugs from dealers then give it to Black to sell, but I think toward the end of Black's life, he must have tried to stop working with the guy and I think he killed Black."

"What? I've heard a lot of shit about Black. I thought that some dudes from L.A. killed Black or some Detroit niggas."

"This guy killed Black."

"How do you know this?"

"I don't know it for sure but I got a hunch he killed Black."

Starr sighed and said, "Okay, Jada, why do I feel like you're leaving something out?"

"Because you know me."

"What are you leaving out?"

"This guy, Barry Daniels, just popped up at my house one day saying that he needed me to get Fresh or Shamari to help him get rid of three kilos," Jada lied. She had actually met him at his office The day he had given her the Beyonce tickets.

"Who the hell is Barry Daniels? What the hell does this have to do with anything?"

"Barry Daniels is the FBI agent, and he had Black's phone. There were some text messages between Black and I. Some shit about hooking up later. I don't know what was I thinking. I was horny as fuck and wanted to see him again."

"Wow and so that's why you think that he killed Black?"

"Yes, though he won't admit it."

"So, you're stressed because he wants you to help him get rid of the coke?"

"I've already helped him, but now he wants me to let him know when Fresh goes out of town to get his work."

"Set him up?"

"No he wants to take his shit."

"Don't do it."

"It's too late. I told him I would help."

"Jada, you absolutely can't let this man take Fresh's work. You could get killed girl."

"I know."

"Go to Fresh and tell him about this dude. Tell him about Black."

"I thought about that but Fresh is on the run and I know this Barry Daniels motherfucker would get him locked up for sure."

"It's just a matter of time before they get Fresh anyway, but you can't do this."

"I know." Jada was ashamed that she agreed to help this man out.

"Jada, I don't want you to get killed."

"Don't say that."

"It's the truth," Starr said. "I need me a drink. This is too much for me to handle."

Jada disappeared into the kitchen then returned with two shots of Patron. The both downed their drinks.

Starr said, "So, what are you going to do?"

"I don't know."

"What made you decide to do this is in the first place?"

"Me and Fresh have been having problems and I found out that he was still fucking around with his baby mama and I got a little vulnerable."

"But you don't do a man like that, Jada. You know the game, just like me. You've been around hustlers all your life. You know that you can't do a man like that. You can't conspire with the police to take his work."

"I know."

"Jada, don't do it."

"But what am I going to do? I told him that I was going to do it."

*****

A big black man with a potato head, wide nose, adorned with a microscopic gold nose ring named Bull jumped Low Down from behind and snatched his ass up and dragged him into a waiting SUV. Bull drove Low Down's ass to a dirt road in the country.

Meanwhile, across town, Rakeem's car was surrounded by goons with guns. He'd tried to reach for his gun that was under the seat but was unsuccessful because he was shot in the shoulder. Later that night, TeTe, Bull, and Big Country brought Low Down and Rakeem to Lake Oconee.

The two men were untied and TeTe said to the two guys, "Do y'all know each other?"

They both answered no that they did not know each other.

"Want to know why you are here?"

Rakeem said, "Look, bitch, I know that you're going to kill me, so why don't you just kill me. I don't want to get into all of that 'do you know why you're here' bullshit. I know this ain't no PTA meeting."

TeTe approached him and he shoved her. "Get the fuck out of my face!"

 Bull picked him up and slammed him on his face.

TeTe said, "Pick him up."

Bull stood him up then TeTe looked at Low Down. "Anything you gotta say?"

"No."

"Okay, one of y'all are responsible for killing my Boo and I intend to find out which one of y'all did it."

Low Down said, "Who the fuck is your Boo?"

Rakeem said, "That clown-ass nigga Black. FYI, bitch, I ain't kill Black."

Low Down laughed and said, "So that's why we're here? You think somebody killed Black? We didn't kill Black, but we was trying to find his ass."

TeTe said, "Okay, we're going to flip a coin and find out who dies first."

Low Down said, "Do what you gotta do, bitch. "He was feeling braver since he'd heard Rakeem talk shit.

TeTe said, "I want you to rope his ass to the back of the Jet Ski."

Country and Bull tied Low Down to the back of the Jet Ski and Bull drove his ass out in the middle of the lake in a speed boat with the rope around his neck. He was kicking and screaming. Bull cut the rope. Low Down choked and gagged with a mouthful of water before he ultimately died.

Then TeTe said to Rakeem, "Since you the one talking all this shit, I got something special for your ass."

There was a pickup truck with a Porta John on the back of it that was filled with shit.

TeTe said, "Bring his ass in here."

Bull and Big Country tied him up and then placed his ass inside the Porta John. Rakeem started hollering until they gagged him and closed the door. Inside the Porta John, the walls were closing in on him and the turds of shit plastered the floor and the walls were making him nauseous. Big Country and Bull flipped the Porta John on its side and rolled it. Inside the Porta John, tears formed in Rakeem's eyes as he tumbled around.

TeTe said, "So you want to talk shit now?"

"Please let me out of here. Please."

TeTe said, "It's amazing how death can bring the fear out in a bitch-ass nigga."

"Look, I'm sorry." He managed to utter despite the gag in his mouth.

They loaded the Porta John on back of the speed boat and drove it out in the middle of the lake. Then they dropped the Porta John into the lake.

*****

TeTe held a party at her house. John was there as well as Jada, Shamari, Ava and Big Ced. There was food and drink. She had catered food and TeTe was celebrating that she had gotten the people that she felt were responsible for killing Black and her beloved sister.

"You did what?" Jada gasped. "Okay, I understand about your sister, but you said yourself, you didn't know who killed Black."
"What difference does that make?"
"It makes a lot of difference."
"Look, all I know is that Black's kids were murdered. His baby mama was murdered. My sister was murdered. Black was murdered. Do you think I give a fuck if I hurt the wrong person? And as far as I'm concerned, everybody I killed deserved it."
Jada was silent as she thought about Daniels—the man that was really responsible for Black's death and he was still walking around.
TeTe approached Jada with a drink in her hand and said, "What difference does it make, sweetheart? We got revenge and we should celebrate."
"We don't know that."
Shamari approached Jada and said, "Why are you so uptight?"
"Look, bruh, you need to go over there with your bitch and quit worrying about why I'm so uptight. I'm leaving," Jada said.
"Bye." TeTe laughed.

Barry Daniels introduced Jada to another agent. The white agent's name was Mark Dumas. He looked to be in his early forties with a slight stomach and a receding hairline. Jada looked nervous because she was nervous. And though she was telling Daniels about some drug run and not a deal, she still didn't feel right about what she was doing. But she was so deep into it, she didn't have a choice.

Daniels said, "Relax, Jada, you're among friends. He paused "So what do you have for me?"
Jada grimaced.
"I need the phone numbers of Shantelle and Fresh."
Jada scrolled though the contacts in her phone and then gave Daniels Fresh's and Shantelle's numbers. He could trace the numbers and maybe use the GPS to track them.
"Okay, I'm going to need to know what day she's leaving and when she's expected to come back," Daniels said.
"I have to find out when she is coming back."
"Could you just spend the night with Fresh when she's on her way back?"
Dumas said, "Remember, we need to know the color, the make, and the model of the car too."

*****

The phone rang and Jada grabbed the phone from the nightstand. It was Shamari. What the fuck could he possibly want at this time of morning? She looked over at the clock that read 6:01 a.m.

"Hello?"
"Hey. Did I catch you at a bad time?"
"What do you think? It's six a.m. and you know I'm not a morning person."

"Is Fresh with you?"

"Shamari, what do you want? I'm in bed." she complained. She didn't want to be too mean to him because she knew she had been very difficult at TeTe's party.

"Hey, I'm on my way to South Carolina with Hunch to handle some business. Can you go to my lawyer's office today and make a payment for me?"

"How much is the payment?"

"Twelve thousand dollars. I can bring it by now if you want."

"That's okay, I'll pay it. You just make sure you pay me back."

"You know I will."

"Is that it?"

"Yeah."

"Be careful."

"You know I will."

"Bye."

*****

Jada, Shantelle, and Fresh met up at IHOP on Ponce de Leon for breakfast. Fresh and Jada had ordered pancakes, eggs, and turkey sausage before discussing the trip.

Jada said to Fresh, "Shantelle doesn't want you to go running and telling Q about the trip. She wants no part of Q. The man tried to kill her."

Shantelle interjected, "Yeah, if Q knows about this trip, I can't go. If he doesn't know that I am making moves for you, I can go."

Fresh ate his food slowly. He didn't like hiding things from Q but Q had hidden things from him and had proven that he could be selfish. He understood Shantelle's point. This deal needed to go smooth then he would surrender to the proper authorities.

"Look, I'm not telling him anything, but don't say anything to Gordo."

Shantelle looked confused. "Who is Gordo?"

"The guy that you have been seeing every time you go to Houston."

"I've met up with a guy that said his name was Pisa."

"Pisa must be a flunky."

"I don't say shit. It's usually me going to the address that you give me and leaving the car. I take an Uber back to the hotel and when they call me, I go get the car and I'm done."

"Stop taking Uber," Fresh said then he ate a sausage link.

"Why?"

"Uber is a record. More specifically, a record that you were at a particular location."

"Right."

"Take a cab. I know it's more expensive but if safer. You pay with cash and nobody knows that you were somewhere in Mexican territory."

"Smart," Jada said.

"Not smart, careful," Fresh said.

"So when is she leaving?" Jada asked.

"Friday, she's going to drive a 2013 blue Ford Fusion. I'll have it delivered to your house tomorrow. Go get it registered to your name and make sure you get the tag."

"Okay, cool."

"What time is the car coming to her house, Fresh?"

Fresh eyed Jada suspiciously. "I think around two p.m."

"Cool."

Fresh passed Shantelle a cell phone with a piece of white tape stuck to the back. On the tape was the number 404 345 0989. "My number is the same as your number except the last digit is an eight."

Jada memorized the numbers. She would text them to Barry Daniels later.

Jada stood and said, "I have to go. I have to go work out and then take care of something for Shamari."

Fresh grabbed her hand and said, "Can I see you later?"

Jada gave him a fake smile and said, "I'd like that."

When Jada strolled into Joey Turch's office, he waved her to a chair in front of his desk as he finished his conversation with a client named Alphonso Tucker. Tucker had eight prior sell and delivery charges and was sentenced to a year in a halfway house. He was cursing Turch out saying that Turch wasn't shit and that he shouldn't have hired him.

"If that's the way you feel, Alphonso. Anyway I have to go, I have a paying client."

Alphonso shouted, "Motherfucker, you act like I don't pay."

Turch terminated the call.

"Damn, he was heated about shit," Jada said.

"You know that's how it is in my business. Can't make everyone happy, although I tried." Turch stood clasping his hands. "Do you know Alphonso Tucker?"

"No."

"Hood trapper that lives on the West Side."

Jada was shocked that Turch was using black lingo but she supposed that he had picked it up from his years of defending drug dealers.

"No, I don't know him."

"He's the type of guy that traps from the time he wakes up at two p.m. until about four in the morning. That's all he does. He has no aspirations to do or be anything else. Well anyway, he's made millions of dollars and he won't leave the hood. All he wants to do is fight pit bulls, smoke weed and listen to trap music. I've gotten charges dismissed for him and thrown out. With this latest charge, he should have been sent to prison, but I got him in a halfway house and all of a sudden I'm the worse lawyer in Atlanta. I ain't shit."

"Can't please them all."

"That's what I say."

It had been a very long time since Jada had seen him and she had almost forgotten how much of a pervert he was until he licked his lips.

"I don't want to spend one more second talking about that guy to you, Jada."

"You remember me?" Jada smiled.

"There aren't many women as beautiful as you are that walk through that door."

Jada blushed and Turch's eyes dropped to her erect nipples piercing through her fuchsia blouse.

"So what brings you here?"

"I'd come to make a final payment for Shamari."

"Oh, I'd almost forgotten about that. But you know, it's not always about money with you and Shamari. We're like old friends. I'm just glad he was released." He lied. He had just spoken to his billing department about Shamari that morning.

She passed him a check for five thousand dollars and the rest in cash.

Joey tucked the money in a drawer underneath the desk. When he reappeared from under the desk, her top button was unbuttoned. Jada said, "It's hot in here."

"You're making it hot in here."

"You're such a flirt."

Joey Turch flashed his wedding band. "Can't a man dream?"

"A long as that's all you're doing. I supposed there is no harm." Jada had very little faith in men. "I gotta go," she said.

She offered him her hand and he held onto it for a long time before letting go. She made a dash toward the door and he eyed her ass in that tight little grey skirt. Commando or G-string, he thought.

Before she could exit, he said, "Hey, that was a shame what happened to Tyrann."

She turned and faced him. "Yeah, I miss him so much."

"Me too, but I knew it was going to be bad news for him when he asked me to ask Barry Daniels to get him out of jail. That dude is the worst of the worst."

"Tell me about it."

"How do you know Barry Daniels?"

It was a question that he, in fact, wanted to know but what he really wanted was to stop that gorgeous ass from leaving the office. He wanted to stare at this incredibly breath-taking woman for the next couple of hours.

She took a seat back down.

*****

A female voice came through Q's speakerphone. "When am I going to get to see you?"

"I don't know," he said. He removed a box of Honey Nut Cheerios from the counter and dumped some into a green cereal bowl. Then he poured some almond milk into the bowl.

The woman said, "Look, you asked me to get you out on bond and I did. I put my name on the line to get yo ass out on bond and all you have been doing is throwing me shade. You know I didn't really have to do it."

"I know and I appreciate what you have done for me. I really do."

"Good. As long as you know that nobody in Atlanta would have gotten yo ass out on bond. You ain't have nobody, but I was there for you."

He ate his cereal.

"You used me," she said.

"I used you. Are you serious?"

"You used me so you could get out and see Starr because you knew that her uppity stank ass wasn't going to get you out. Hell, you couldn't even call her when you was in there."

He chewed cereal.

"Q, you're smacking in my ear; you're being rude as a motherfucker."

He set the cereal spoon down. "How much money do you want?"

"You know what we discussed."

"What did we discuss?"

"Since you want to play stupid, I'm calling the bondsman tomorrow to ask him to take my name off the goddamned bond. Maybe that will refresh your memory."

"Don't do that."

88

"You know what I want. Why are you playing games with me? You know what the deal was. I don't see why you're acting like that."
"Look, come by my place Friday night and I'll have thirty thousand dollars in cash for you."
"Fifty thousand."
"Look, you said thirty."
"Thirty was the agreement before I realized that you were going to play these childish-ass games."
"Come by at 7:30 and I'll have the money."
"I have something to do at 7:30. I can come by at eight."

*****

Shamari introduced Stunna to TeTe and John. They sat at TeTe's kitchen table. Stunna was eyeing TeTe, not in a sexual way, but in admiration. Shamari had given him the backstory about how she ran her operation and how she had been Black's girlfriend before he was murdered.

She was in her forties, but he was loving her style. The classy pantsuit and the jewels and, damn, she was smelling savory. She was a boss for sure.
Shamari said, "I was telling Stunna about how you believed that this FBI agent had something to do with Black's murder, but you just couldn't put your finger on it."
"Yeah, I really believe that." TeTe paused then turned to face Shamari and said, "I know you said Silky was okay."
Stunna frowned. "Who the hell is Silky?"
"What is your name again, sir?"
"Stunna."
"Oh, my bad, Stunna, I know you said that Stunna was okay and I do believe that he is. I get good vibes about people, but the point I'm trying to make is, why are we telling him what we believe? Are you down to help us?"
"I'm here to help myself."
TeTe narrowed her eyes. "And what does that mean?"
"I think this is the same motherfucker that took my work."
"Oh yeah, how do you know he took your work?"

89

"The description of him. He was with some skinny-ass white dude and he is big and bald with a beard. Shamari said that the motherfucker was going around hitting up D-boys in Atlanta, taking their shit and putting it back on the street. So I want to get his ass."

TeTe said, "I've been told I was nuts, but taking out an FBI agent is out there."

"Look, the motherfucker is dirty. I mean we can do this shit smoothly. Maybe you can put one of your bitches on him and get him to come back to her house. Then I'll send somebody in there to take him out."

"What about the girl?"

"Fuck her, she's going to have to take one for the team."

"Look, Stunna," TeTe said, "I know you're upset about your product—"

 He cut her off. "You damn right I am and I'm going to do something about it. I'm not going to sit here and just have a whole bunch of meetings and shit. I don't give a fuck. If someone crosses me; they have to pay."

TeTe threw her hands up. "Shamari, take your friend away. I can't talk to him. This shit is not making any sense."

Stunna took several deep breaths to calm himself down and when he was calm, he said, "Ms. TeTe, I apologize for acting an ass in your house, but I'm pissed right now and what you're saying is the truth. I have to make better plans."

"Look, let's forget that plan."

John said, "I don't think we have to abandon the plan. Feds get killed all the time, but I don't think Stunna should do it. I've got a guy who can do it who's a professional. This will be much better than some street thugs that might drop a receipt or do something stupid and get caught and give us all up."

"Damn right," TeTe said.

Stunna said, "Let's do it. When can you call the dude and when can he do the hit?"

"First let me get the address and then I'll call my guy and get him to do it."

Goldie called Micky back to back and said that one of the guys that was with the dude that had raped her was in the club. Micky called Stunna and Blue and the rest of his crew. Shamari called Big Ced and his boys and they were all in Magic City in the VIP section. Goldie came over and Stunna ordered a bottle of champagne — a requirement for the VIP section.

Stunna approached Goldie and asked, "Okay, where is the motherfucker that raped my sister?"

She said, "Well, he was here that night." She pointed to a chubby pie-faced man with a pleasant demeanor.

Micky saw the man and recognized him. "Yeah, he was there that night, but he didn't rape me. He didn't go back to the house. But I did see him with the niggas that raped me earlier at the club."

Stunna climbed over the rope that separated the two VIP sections and made eye contact with the man. Then he asked if he could have a word with him. The man approached Stunna and they shook hands.

"Look, bruh, I don't know you and you don't know me," Stunna said.

The man looked confused and he said, "Okay."

 "You see that girl over there?" He pointed to Micky who was downing a bottle of champagne.

"The one that looks like a dude?"

"That's my sister, homie."

"Okay, my bad. I ain't know."

"A few weeks ago she was in this club and she was arguing with a dude and she said that you were with the guy."

The man looked confused and then he said, "Oh yeah, I do remember that. She was arguing with this dude named New York."

"New York?"

"I mean, I don't really know him like that, but I see him from time to time."

"You know how to get in touch with him?"

The waitress approached the man and said, "Y'all going to need to buy another bottle or get out of the section."

He looked at Stunna and said, "We're going out of here. I can't afford another bottle."

Stunna passed the woman five hundred dollars and got them two more bottles.

"Thanks."

"No problem. What's your name?"

"Gerome."

"Okay, Gerome, you seem like a nice dude. I'm guessing you're not a hustler."

"No man, I'm a computer programmer and I just came out to have a good time. Me and the boys. We all pitched in to get a bottle."

"Back to New York."

"Yeah?"

"What do you know about him?"

"He hangs with my cousin Teddy I don't see them too often."

The waitress dropped the two bottles on Gerome's table.

"This is what I'm going to need you to do, Gerome. I'm going to need you to contact your cousin or give me his address."

Gerome's nose wrinkled. "So what is this about?"

"My sister got raped that night and you just so happened to be with the niggas that did it. So either you tell us where your cousin live or you die tonight, Gerome. It's your choice. I'll make it easy for you, tell me how to find your cousin and I buy you two more bottles or I pour two bottles on your burned body."

Gerome said, "He lives in Cumberland."

"He's your cousin, right?"

"Yes."

"Text him and ask him for his address. Tell him that you're coming over tonight."

Gerome removed his phone from his pocket and sent his cousin a text through WhatsApp.

Gerome: CUZO, WHAT'S YOUR ADDRESS? I'M GOING TO GET UBER TO DROP ME OFF.

Teddy: 1345 COBB GALLERIA PARKWAY AND BRING SOME HENNY, NIGGA.

Stunna patted Gerome on the back. "Now I'm going to need for you to give me your cellphone and I'm going to give it to one of my guys," Stunna said as he pointed to a black ugly motherfucker named Taj. "Taj is going to give you your phone when he gets word from me. Okay."
Gerome passed Stunna his phone.
Then he patted him on the back again and said. "You did the right thing. Good luck with work in the morning." He winked.
"I don't know if I'm going."
Stunna shot him a fake smile and said, "Well, at least you're not going to hell tonight."

*****

The thunder roared and lightening crackled then followed by the ding of the doorbell. Fresh tiptoed to the peephole. He was on the lam after all, so he had to be careful. He was surprised when he saw that it was Jada standing on the other side of the door, holding a red and yellow umbrella. He opened the door and they stared at one another for a moment before he invited her in.

She took a step inside and he closed the door behind her and he said, "So, what brings you here?"
"You said you wanted to see me the other day. You don't want me here?"
"Of course, but I didn't really think you would come."
"Why not?"
"I thought you were over me."
"I can't get over someone I care about that fast."
"You care about me?"
"Of course I do. I love you, Fresh." She did love him and she hated that she was spying for Barry Daniels. She didn't want him to take Fresh's product. More than that, she had hoped that he would keep his word and not take Fresh to jail.
"I missed you."
"I missed you, too," she said then she dropped the umbrella and approached him and took him into her arms.

"You're wet," he said.

She laughed and said, "Duh! It is raining outside. It's storming."

"I know. Well you can take those wet clothes off and slide into one of my tees if you want."

"I'd like that," She said before disappearing into the back and remerging with a T-shirt and that was it.

When she returned, he was face to face with her kitty. "Damn, you sure know how to make a brother weak."

"A brother?"

"That's what I am."

"Fresh, you're a nigga."

He laughed and said, "Well, you sure do know how to make a nigga weak."

"How?"

His eyes zeroed in on her shaven kitty. She crossed her legs and he made a sad face.

"She don't like you anymore," Jada referred to womanhood in the third person.

"She loves me. I'm her best friend."

"She says that you can't be faithful."

"I can be faithful and I will."

Jada laughed and said, "The lies that men tell when they want some kitty."

"You think I want your kitty?"

"Not think." she smiled, "I know."

She strolled past then flashed her VJ at Fresh so that he could see the lips.

"Jada, why are you doing me like this?" He kicked his shoes off and removed his socks. Barefoot on the wooden floors, he approached her. His iPhone buzzed.

 "Aren't you going to check that?" She asked.

"That can wait."

"Check it, babe. It might be Shantelle."

"Right." He picked up the phone; Shantelle was calling.

"Hello?"

"It's me," Shantelle said.

"Hey, where are you?"

"I'm in Dallas. I'll be in Birmingham in eight or nine hours."

"You okay?"
"Everything is great. It's raining and I like to move when it rains
because I'm less likely to get stopped."
"Exactly."
"Check with me every two hours."
"Okay."
The call ended. His penis was now limp.
Jada said, "That was Shantelle, right?"
"Yes."
"Where was she?"
"Dallas."
"Okay, so she should get here in about eleven or twelve hours?"
Fresh raised his eyebrows. "Yeah."
She kneeled, and took him inside her mouth, grabbing his hand
and placing it on the back of her head. She came up and gasped
for air. "Play some music, you know I love music."
He grabbed his phone and connected it to the Beats Pill. Bryson
Tiller's DON'T came through the speakers.
She said, "Can you put it on something else?"
"What's the matter? You don't like the song?"
"I do, but I'd rather listen to something else. They've been playing
that song to death. Put it on some old school shit like Jodeci. I love
that 90s music."
FEENIN' played through the Bluetooth speaker and Jada was back
on her knees.
He stood her up "I want to taste you."
She made her way over to the sofa and bent over then placed her
hands on the sofa back. He lay on his back.
"Sit on my face," he said.
She smiled wondering if he was serious. She'd never had a man
tell her to sit on his face. Of course, there were guys saying that
they wanted her to sit on their face.
She hesitated. He grabbed her waist and pulled her down until he
was inches from her kitty. He French kissed her slit. She trembled
as she straddled his face. Love juices dripped into his mouth. His
tongue moved in and out of her pleasure center. She screamed;
tried to escape. He wrestled her and tossed her on her stomach.
He continued to kiss her wetness. She held on to the couch until

his tongue intruded into her ass crack, she tried to crawl up the wall. She clawed the paint on the wall. This nigga made her feel amazing.

She turned and faced him then removed his T-shirt, tossed it onto the floor. His chest against her breasts, she felt his heartbeat and she could smell the garlic on his breath from the spaghetti-lunch he'd enjoyed. Their tongue's wrestled and she said, "I want to take you in my mouth. Force it down my throat. Rape me."

He narrowed his eyes.

"Take it, Fresh. It's yours."

He forced himself inside her, and she said, "Take me."

She could feel him inside her. Her fingers dug into his back and she nibbled on his ear. She said, "Cum in my mouth. I want to taste you."

"No. I can't do that."

"I want you to."

He kept stroking until he climaxed. She turned him over and he was now sitting on the sofa. She rode him reverse cowboy and when she exploded on his legs, she turned and she wrestled with him to take possession of his penis.

Two hours later, she showered. Fresh was still asleep. She phoned Shantelle then called Barry Daniels to give him Shantelle's whereabouts. She would be traveling through Birmingham on I-20.

*****

It was 1:13 in the morning when Stunna and Blue buzzed the apartment. A woman's voice came over the intercom and asked if he was Gerome.

"Yeah, it's me."

"The door is open."

She let them in the building.

Stunna and Blue tiptoed through the kitchen and determined that there were only two bedrooms in the apartment. Teddy was applying KY jelly to his girlfriend Toya's ass when he heard the commotion in the room. "Is that you, cuzo?" Teddy said.

Blue said, "Yeah."

"Okay, go head and watch some TV. I got the jail broken Firestick,
so watch a movie or something till I come out."
Blue said, "Aight." Seconds later, Blue turned the doorknob of the
bedroom door to see if it was locked. It was so he kicked the
fuckin' hinges off the door just as Teddy had entered his girlfriend
from behind.
Three-month-old ShatiraShatima Michaels was lying in a bassinet
and when she heard the commotion, she started crying. Blue
glanced over at the baby. She was wearing a onesie with I LOVE
DADDY on the front. The decision was easy—pick the baby up.
Blue picked the baby up and held her, rocking her trying to calm
her down. When Teddy rotated in the bed and saw the strange
men in his house, he said. "What the fuck?"
Stunna said, "Look, you have one decision to make. Let me know
where the motherfucker that raped my sister is or your baby is
going out of the goddamned window."
Toya stood up, screaming. The KY jelly quickly drying in her ass
crack. "What are they talking about?"
"Tell me where the fuck New York lives and your baby lives. If not,
Blue is going to see if this pretty little angel can fly. I have kids of
my own, so I don't want to have to do this, but you best believe if
you don't tell me how the fuck I can get in touch with New York,
this baby is going to go out of the window head first."
Pretty, little ShatiraShatima sensed something was wrong and she
started to cry. She peed in Blue's arms. Blue held the baby
outward and a stream of yellow piss rolled down his arm.
"I knew New York was bad fucking news. I don't understand why
you was hanging out with this clown in the first place. Look, I'll tell
you where New York lives, just don't harm my baby," Toya said.
Stunna turned to Blue. "Put the baby down."
Blue put ShatiraShatima down in the bassinet and the pretty little
angel dozed. Stunna stood over the baby and he thought about his
own kids. Then he looked at the naked woman and her coward-ass
boyfriend who stood with a blanket covering his tiny dick.
Stunna said, "You lucky I have a soft spot for babies or else this
baby would be without a father."
Toya said, "He's not my baby father."
"What?"

"No."
Blue removed his gun, aimed it at Teddy and said, "I'm going to give you three seconds to jump out the window or I'm shooting you in the head."
"I'm naked."
"You think I can't see that?"
The man encased himself in the blanket like a cocoon.
Blue laughed and said, "Drop the blanket."
Teddy dropped the blanket. His tiny dick had shriveled up into his navel.
"I'm going to die. Look, I want to tell you something about New York."
"We already have the address, we don't need you." Stunna said.
"Oh yeah, but I bet you didn't know that your sister was set up? She was set up by her girl."
Stunna looked at Blue then back at Teddy. "Who was it?"
"A chick named Kelsey."
"Kelsey?" Stunna approached the man and slapped him in the face with his gun. "Quit lying, motherfucker. Kelsey was with her the night it happened."
"I'm telling you, bruh. It was Kelsey. She told us what time she would be at the club and all. She's been fucking around with New York and she got mad at New York because he approached your sister at the club. She didn't want New York's face to be familiar to your sister because she thought the shit was going to come back to her."
Tiny-dick Teddy was trembling but Stunna still didn't know if he believed him. Kelsey had been around his family for a while.
Teddy said, "I know that you lost some work recently and there were two Feds that took your product from your UPS driver."
"Yeah, how do you know that?"
"That was me and a white boy named Robbie posing as Feds. We took the work because your sister had told Kelsey and Kelsey told New York."
Blue said, "He ain't lying, bruh."
"No, I'm not lying. Just don't kill me. Can I show you something else?"
"What?"

"Follow me." Teddy walked through the door. Stunna followed and Blue kept his eye on Toya and the baby. When they were in the guest room, Teddy opened the closet and then dug into a plastic storage container. He handed Stunna two bricks of coke and some cash and showed him the badges that he and the white boy had used.

"Motherfucker," Stunna said.

"I'm telling you that girl Kelsey ain't shit."

Stunna walked over toward the container and said, "What else is in there?"

"Nothing. I've given you the money and the work. The only thing left is two bulletproof vests."

Stunna ordered Teddy to get the fuck out of the way. He searched the container and found two black body armor vests, several rounds of ammunition and fake DEA and FBI badges. He knew then he had to kill Kelsey.

Stunna called Blue into the room and ordered him to tie Toya up. They gave the baby a warm bottle of milk before they walked out of the door with Teddy.

CHAPTER 17

Agent Daniels and two other agents were staked out near the I-20 coming from Birmingham. They'd notified the troopers to be on the lookout for a blue Ford Fusion. Torrential rain fell as if God was standing in the heavens dumping buckets of water down on Atlanta. And the traffic was moving at a snail's pace. Nobody wanted to drive or get hurt. It was around 3:24 a.m. when one of the agents received a call saying that the car had been spotted. It was about twenty-five minutes out of Atlanta and at approximately 4:08 a.m., they saw the car. Daniels, who was driving, trailed the car for about ten miles before igniting his siren and the car pulled onto the side of the road.

Daniels was right behind her. He had activated a light so that he could see into the car. His wipers were on full blast. He notified his crew by radio, giving them instructions that he would approach her alone. There would be no need for weapons or false bravado. This was a young girl. He would speak to her gently and flash his FBI credentials then tell her that someone had given her up. He would convince her that the best thing for her to do was to tell him where the drugs were.

He wouldn't try to convince her to give up the connect and he wouldn't follow her to deliver the drugs. He'd tell her to just give him the drugs and everything would be cool. He knew that when given this choice, any logical human being would do this. He would let her go and convince her that he would protect her from Fresh, which would be a lie. After he got what he wanted, he wouldn't give a fuck about what Fresh did to her.

He powered off his ignition and stepped out into a puddle of water. His Levi's and his Pumas were soaked, but there was no time to worry about that. There was lots of coke in the car, probably in the door panel. Stupid-ass drug dealers were still thinking that was a good place to hide drugs in 2016. His footsteps squished as he walked slowly to the car. When he got to the car, he couldn't see the woman's face clearly because of the rain. She was on the phone talking to someone. He'd heard her say what mile marker she was at.

She said, "I think I'm going to jail—"

Daniels tapped on the window and said, "Get off the phone right now."

*****

Stunna held his gun against Teddy's temple and made him lead him to New York's home in Dunwoody. When the bell rang, New York looked into the living room from the kitchen. The front door was only a few feet away. New York was making some cheese eggs and steak and was about to get into bed to watch the season finale of Game of Thrones.

"Who is it?"

"It's me, Teddy."

New York picked up his iPhone and used his Alarm app to verify that it was Teddy. It was indeed Teddy but there were two men behind him. He could see one holding a gun to Teddy's back.

The bell rung again.

New York said, "Just a minute." He sprinted to the bedroom and retrieved a silver Taurus 9.mm from the junk drawer next to his bed. As he was about to re-enter the kitchen, he heard the hinges break off the door. He took a step in the hallway and fired three shots. Two hit Teddy in the chest and the third one hit Stunna in the stomach--he collapsed. New York ran to the back of the apartment and jumped out of the window. Blue was too slow. He came back to attend to Stunna. Teddy was lying in a pool of blood already dead.

*****

It was 8:30 Friday night and Q was cooking a turkey burger on his Foreman grill when he received a call from the concierge saying that he had a guest. He removed the burgers from the

101

Foreman grill and placed them on a plate. Seconds later, he opened the door and Meeka walked in.

She was looking around the place and she said, "So, this is how the motherfuckin' cheese and wine crowd live?"
Q closed the door behind her.
She was dressed in jeans, heels, and a blazer. She looked very nice as if she might have been going on a date.
He said, "Looking good. Meeka."
"Thank you." She smiled and she was looking very nice. She followed him into the kitchen and he offered her a turkey burger.
"I don't eat that bourgeoisie shit."
"A turkey is--?" Q looked confused.
"You got any Mac n Cheese in this motherfucka, some ribs, some lemon pepper wangs? That's what I like, nigga." She sat at the table and then she said, "I ain't come here for all of that anyway. Do you got my money?"
"Yeah, I got your money."
"Get it please, sir. Mama got shit to do and the last thing I need is my sister to come see me up in yo' spot."
"Your sister ain't fucking with me."
"You haven't seen her?"
"I did and she don't want anything to do with me."
Meeka spotted a bottle on the counter.
She stood and invited herself to a glass then asked, "Do you mind?"
"It's too late now."
"Well, I know you ain't got nothing to smoke in this motherfucker." She walked over to the side of the room and admired the floor to ceiling glass. "This is some nice shit. This is my first time in a penthouse. I can see Turner Field. This is what I call living. I need to find me a kingpin so I be in some shit like this." She downed the liquor and poured another glass. "Q, I need my money."
Q walked back to the bedroom and reappeared with a brown grocery bag full of cash. He passed it to her and said, "It's all there. Thirty thousand dollars."
Meeka frowned and said, "Don't play with me, Q."

He grinned and said, "It's fifty thousand dollars and I appreciate what you did for me. I know it was a hard thing to do."

"Thank you because Lord knows I could use the bread."

Q was standing over by the kitchen counter applying some mustard on his burger. Then he sliced a tomato. When he finished, he turned to find Meeka standing naked in the middle of the kitchen.

"What are you doing?"

"Penetrate me now."

He set his sandwich on the counter as he scanned her body. The skin, the curves, and the teeth were all like her sister's. Meeka had a phenomenal body for a woman in her late thirties and Q was aroused as he tried not to stare at Meeka who had this come-hither-look.

She said, "Come on, Q. Fuck me. Fuck me or I'm calling the goddamn bondsman."

www.ingramcontent.com/pod-product-compliance
Lightning Source LLC
Chambersburg PA
CBHW070258120726
47910CB00007B/2297